The Prodigal's Christmas Reunion

Kathryn Springer

Love Inspired

Special thanks and acknowledgment to Kathryn Springer for her participation in the Rocky Mountain Heirs miniseries.

Recycling programs for this product may not exist in your area.

™ LOVE INSPIRED BOOKS

ISBN-13: 978-0-373-81589-0

THE PRODIGAL'S CHRISTMAS REUNION

Copyright © 2011 by Harlequin Books S.A.

www.LoveInspiredBooks.com

Printed in U.S.A.

An adorable preschool-age boy came in the barn.

A bright red snowsuit enveloped his thin frame but instead of a stocking cap, a cowboy hat was perched on his head. A battered black Stetson that looked a lot like the one Lucas used to wear.

He smiled shyly, pressed his cheek against Lucas's leg and pointed to the foal. "Thatsa baby horse."

Erin couldn't help but smile back.

"This is Max," Lucas said.

"Hey, Max. I'm Erin. It's nice to meet you. Do you like horses?"

"I like trucks better," Max declared.

"We'll have to work on that." Erin winked at the boy. "So, who does this little cowboy belong to?" she asked Lucas.

"He belongs to me," Lucas said.

Rocky Mountain Heirs:
When the greatest fortune of all is love.

Books by Kathryn Springer

Love Inspired

Tested by Fire
Her Christmas Wish
By Her Side
For Her Son's Love
A Treasure Worth Keeping
Hidden Treasures
Family Treasures
Jingle Bell Babies
*A Place to Call Home
*Love Finds a Home
*The Prodigal Comes Home
The Prodigal's Christmas Reunion

*Mirror Lake

Steeple Hill

Front Porch Princess
Hearts Evergreen
  "A Match Made for
  Christmas"
Picket Fence Promises
The Prince Charming List

KATHRYN SPRINGER

is a lifelong Wisconsin resident. Growing up in a "newspaper" family, she spent long hours as a child plunking out stories on her mother's typewriter and hasn't stopped writing since! She loves to write inspirational romance because it allows her to combine her faith in God with her love of a happy ending.

Lord, you have assigned me my portion and my cup; You have made my lot secure. The boundary lines have fallen for me in pleasant places; surely I have a delightful inheritance.
—*Psalms* 16:5–6

This book is dedicated to Linda, Arlene, Lenora,
Carolyne and Roxanne—
an amazing, gifted group of authors it was
a pleasure to work with. Your encouragement,
prayers and unfailing patience were a blessing!

Chapter One

Lucas Clayton could have driven down the streets of his hometown blindfolded.

The thought was tempting.

Because not even a moonless night and the light snow sifting onto the windshield of his pickup could conceal the silhouettes of the businesses that sagged against each other in a tired line along Railroad Street.

Jones Feed and Supply. The grocery store. The post office.

Each building held more than just sacks of grain or canned goods or stamps. Each one held a memory. Or two.

Or a hundred.

The town of Clayton, Colorado might have been named after one of his dusty ancestors, but Lucas had never taken any pride in that. Growing up, having the last name Clayton had only been one more expectation weighing him down. One more invisible shackle holding him in place.

Lucas had broken free at eighteen and left home with a beat-up canvas duffel bag, a chip on his shoulder as solid as a chunk of rock hewn from the Rockies themselves and a vow never to return.

As he traveled from job to job, eventually landing in Georgia, both the duffel bag *and* the chip on his shoulder had remained constant companions.

But now, after seven years, he'd broken the vow. Not that he'd had a choice.

His grandfather, George Clayton Sr., had passed away during the summer, leaving behind a will that had caused new splits in an already fractured family. George's brother, Samuel, and his offspring had made life unbearable for years, but they stood to inherit everything—if Lucas and his five cousins didn't satisfy the conditions of the will.

That didn't surprise him. Leave it to good old Grandpa George to attempt to control people's lives from the grave—he'd certainly made a habit of it while he'd been alive. As a lawyer, George Clayton had a reputation for being ruthless, manipulative and self-serving. As a grandfather, he hadn't been a whole lot better.

Lucas still couldn't believe his cousins had agreed to put their lives on hold and return to Clayton for a whole year. But he was the last one to return.

Lucas hadn't exactly had a choice about that, either.

A promise made to a dying friend had taken him

to places that no sane person would have chosen to go, but loyalty to his sister had brought him back to Clayton.

Cruising through the lone signal light at the intersection, Lucas saw a soft glow in one of the windows farther down the street.

He didn't even have to read the faded sign above the door to know which one it was.

The Cowboy Café.

Lucas struggled against a memory that fought its way to the surface. And lost.

An image of a girl's face materialized in front of him, clear as a photograph. A heart-shaped face. Hair that glowed like the embers in a campfire, shades of bronze and copper lit with strands of gold. Wide brown eyes that had a disconcerting tendency to see straight into his soul.

Lucas's fingers bit into the steering wheel.

He couldn't think about Erin Fields.

Wouldn't think about her.

She'd made her choice. Before he'd left, Lucas had asked Erin to go with him but she'd refused, choosing loyalty to her family over her love for him.

Maybe she'd been willing to put her dreams and her future on hold, but Lucas knew he wouldn't *have* a future if he stayed in Clayton. The confines of the small town would have served as a mold, shaping him into something—someone—he didn't want to be.

His father.

Vern Clayton, medical missionary and well-respected pillar of the church and the community, had died in a car accident when Lucas was a teenager, but his mother had insisted he follow in his father's footsteps by serving God and becoming a doctor.

Instead, Lucas had turned his back on both.

Disappointing people seemed to be his gift.

As if to underscore the point, an image of Erin's tear-streaked face returned. He could almost feel the touch of her hand on his.

I'll always love you, Lucas. And I'll wait for you.

Lucas pushed the memory aside.

He'd be crazy to think Erin had stayed true to the promise she'd made that night. They'd been kids. That kind of vow didn't stand the test of time.

From his experience, not a whole lot did.

Turning onto a side street, he pulled up to the third house on the left. Completely dark. Lucas hadn't expected a welcoming committee—especially when he hadn't told his mother or Mei the exact date of his arrival.

Lucas's fingers curled around the keys in the ignition, fighting the temptation to shift the truck into Drive and take off into the night. The way he had seven years ago...

A soft rustle came from the backseat.

Twisting around, Lucas summoned what he hoped was a reassuring smile. "It's okay, Max."

A pair of hazel eyes blinked at him from the shadows. "Daddy?" came the sleepy response.

Lucas's throat tightened, preventing him from responding.

Not that he even knew *how* to respond.

For the past few months, he'd provided the little boy with food and shelter. The basic necessities. What he hadn't been able to give Max Cahill was the thing he needed the most. His parents.

What were you thinking, Scott?

His former college roommate hadn't been. That was the problem. Scott's addictions had led him down a path that had ultimately cost him his life— and if Lucas hadn't stepped in, the life of an innocent child.

Max lifted his arms toward Lucas and grinned. "We gettin' out now?"

Lucas shook his head. They'd been on the road for more than forty-eight hours and yet his pint-size passenger, who recently turned four, somehow managed to display a more cheerful disposition than the driver.

"Yup. We're getting out now."

"French fries?" Max stifled a yawn even as his eyes brightened with hope.

"I can't make any promises, buddy." And there we have it, Lucas thought. Another one of his flaws exposed.

A raw December wind stung Lucas's face as he

hopped out of the truck cab. The crisp temperatures and falling snow felt almost surreal after traipsing through the Florida Everglades, dodging the men who had killed Scott Cahill. Unbuckling the booster seat, he scooped Max into his arms, blankets and all.

The boy burrowed against him and Lucas felt a familiar burst of panic. The one that gripped him whenever Max turned to him for comfort.

Lucas anchored Max against his chest with one arm while fishing for the spare house key his mom always stashed behind the mailbox. Before he had a chance to slide it into the lock, the porch light came on.

He had only a second to react before the front door swung open and a petite, dark haired whirlwind launched herself at him.

"Lucas! You're home."

"Home," came a muffled chirp from inside the cocoon of blankets.

Mei's astonished gaze dropped to the quilt. Lucas could see the question in his adopted sister's ebony eyes and knew exactly what she was thinking.

He'd given Jack McCord, his sister's new love who'd tracked him down in Florida, permission to offer the family an abbreviated version of what he'd gone through to retrieve Max from the thugs who'd snatched him away from his dying father during a drug deal gone bad. But judging from the expression on Mei's face, they had expected Lucas to return to Clayton alone.

And why wouldn't they? an inner voice mocked him.

He'd been MIA for years, communicating with his family through emails and the occasional phone call. That way, he stayed in control of the relationships.

It was a little unsettling to admit that maybe, just maybe, he and Grandpa George had something in common other than their DNA.

"Hey, Erin, I'm supposed to let you know that we're getting a little low on ground beef..."

Erin Fields jumped at the sound of a voice behind her.

She pasted on a smile to cover the guilty look on her face before turning around to face Kylie Jones. Which was a little ridiculous, given the fact that it wasn't a crime to be caught putting on your coat.

Unless it was the middle of the day.

And your name was Erin Fields.

Kylie zeroed in on the coat clutched in her hands. And then her gaze shifted to the clock on the wall.

"The lunch crowd is thinning out so I thought I'd leave early," Erin explained.

"You're leaving. Early." The waitress repeated, her green eyes widening in disbelief.

Maybe because Erin never left early. As the

owner of the café, she was the first one to arrive in the morning and the last one to leave at night.

"Only a few hours." Erin winced at the defensiveness that crept into her tone.

She never got defensive, either.

Kylie tipped her head. The movement sent a tumble of light brown curls over one shoulder. "Is everything all right?" she asked hesitantly. "You've been a little...distracted...lately."

Lately being the past forty-eight hours, Erin thought. And if pressed, she could take it a step further and pinpoint the exact moment it had started. When she'd overheard a customer casually mention that Lucas Clayton was back in town.

As much as Erin had both dreamed of and dreaded the possibility of that happening, nothing had prepared her for the reality.

Lucas. In Clayton. For a year.

Erin knew all about the conditions of George Sr.'s will.

It had been the talk of the town since July. One by one, the Clayton cousins had returned to their roots—all except Lucas.

Every time the bells above the door of the café jingled, Erin's nerves would jingle right along with them. It didn't matter that the logical side of her brain knew he wouldn't seek her out. When it came to Lucas Clayton, the hopeful side had always prevailed.

Which proved she still hadn't learned her lesson.

Which, in turn, made her pathetic.

Harboring feelings for a guy who'd claimed to be in love with her—and then left without a backward glance.

Erin was tempted to confide in Kylie, but even now, after all these years, it felt as if she would be breaking a promise. At Lucas's request they'd kept their high-school romance a secret from friends and family. He'd claimed he didn't want his reputation to cast a shadow on her and Erin had reluctantly agreed, afraid her mother wouldn't approve of her dating that "wild Clayton boy."

Even when the truth about their relationship would have squelched the malicious rumor that Vincent Clayton, Lucas's cousin, had started about him and Susie Tansley, Lucas had held Erin to that promise. That's when she'd started to wonder if there was another reason he had insisted on keeping their relationship a secret. A reason that had more to do with his being ashamed of *her* than some of the things he'd done…

Kylie snapped her fingers two inches from Erin's nose. "See what I mean? *Distracted.*"

"I'm fine. Really." Even as she said the words, Erin wondered who she was trying to convince. Kylie? Or herself? "It's Diamond I'm worried about. She seemed a little agitated this morning before I left for work, and she's due to drop her foal any day now. I'd feel better if I checked on her." It was the truth—and a legitimate reason to escape the memories pressing down on her.

"You're such a softie." Kylie chuckled. "You treat those animals of yours like children."

Erin knew her friend was teasing but the words still stung. She was twenty-five years old. Her friends were either engaged or already married and starting a family, something she'd always dreamed of.

With Lucas.

Stop.

For Kylie's benefit, Erin mustered a smile. "So, I'll leave everything in your capable hands for a few hours."

Kylie reeled her in for a quick hug. "Don't worry about coming back to close up. I'll take care of it."

"We got six hours 'til then." A gravelly voice snarled from the kitchen. "So how about you take care of the orders piling up in here before you talk about shutting the place down for the night?"

"Be right there, Jerome," Kylie sang out. Lowering her voice, she winked at Erin over her shoulder. "From the way that man carries on, you'd think he's the one who signs my paychecks, not you."

The two women exchanged a grin. Everyone in town knew the old cook's bark was worse than his bite.

"I'll see you tomorrow, then." Erin shrugged on her coat and shook her ponytail free from the sheepskin collar. "And Kylie…thanks."

"No problem. Zach is meeting me here after he gets off work. He claims he can't pass up one of Gerald and Jerome's famous barbecue rib dinners, but I have a hunch he wants to keep an eye on me." Kylie's expression clouded. "Now that Lucas is back in town, Zach thinks it's going to rile up Vincent and the rest of his family even more."

Erin kept her expression neutral, although her heart plummeted at the mention of Lucas's name. "Samuel's side of the family has always enjoyed causing trouble," she murmured.

"You're telling me." Kylie couldn't suppress a shudder. "I almost married into it. I thank God every day that He saved me from making a huge mistake—and brought Zach into my life."

So did Erin. Zach Clayton, the second of the cousins to return to Clayton after the reading of the will, treated Kylie the way she deserved to be treated. With love and respect. Unlike Vincent, who Kylie had caught kissing another woman on the day they were supposed to exchange their vows.

"Vincent can put on quite a show." No matter how many times he'd denied it, Erin had known that Vincent, George Sr.'s nephew, had been behind Susie Tansley's attempt to destroy Lucas's already shaky reputation by claiming he was the father of her unborn baby.

Erin hadn't believed the malicious rumors flying around town about Lucas's relationship with Susie, but Lisette Clayton did. The fact that his own mother hadn't believed the truth had finally pushed Lucas over the edge. By the time the truth came out and Susie's claim had proved to be a lie, the damage had been done.

He'd shown up at Erin's house a little after midnight with a beat-up duffel bag, eyes dark with pain and a reckless offer that had quickly deteriorated into their first—and last—argument.

In the end, Erin had watched Lucas drive away, praying with all her heart that he would change his mind and stay in Clayton. And stand up to the people who'd spread rumors about him.

She'd watched the brake lights on his truck glow red at the stop sign. Left would take him home. Right would take him out of the city limits. He'd turned right.

Toward his dreams. And away from her.

"...Better get back to work before Jerome fires me." Kylie's teasing voice tugged Erin back to the present as she breezed toward the door of the office.

Erin's heart clenched as she followed Kylie into the dining room and her gaze swept from table to table.

Be strong, she silently lectured herself.

Clayton boasted a population of less than a thousand people. Eventually, she and Lucas were going to come face-to-face.

And when they did, Erin knew exactly what she would do. She would hold her head up high and look him right in the eye. Her polite smile would show

Lucas that she was doing all right. She'd moved on, too.

He'd never have to know that he'd taken her heart with him when he left.

Chapter Two

"Easy girl." Erin ran a soothing hand over the flank of the mare stretched out on the floor of the stall. "Hang in there and you'll be a momma in no time."

The horse thrashed weakly in response to the sound of her voice, and Erin felt needle-sharp tears poke at the back of her eyes.

Where was Tweed?

She'd put in an emergency call to the local large animal vet over an hour ago.

Maybe she'd been running away at the time, but Erin was glad she'd left the café early because the moment she'd arrived home from work, she'd known something was wrong. Winston, her corgi, had been standing at the door of the barn instead of ambling down to the mailbox to greet her the way she usually did.

Erin had discovered Diamond lying down in the

stall, already in the throes of what looked as if it were going to be a long and difficult labor.

The blue roan was Erin's first rescue. She'd attended an auction one summer afternoon and spotted the horse tied to the back of a rusty trailer, half-starved and abused. One look into those sorrowful, liquid brown eyes and she couldn't walk away. No one had bothered to mention the mare was expecting.

Even with a good diet, a warm place to sleep and daily doses of tender loving care, Diamond had been slow to regain her strength. Erin had been afraid all along that the horse wouldn't be able to handle a difficult birth. She'd shared her concern with Dr. "Tweed" Brighton, who'd promised to help deliver the foal if necessary.

If only she could get in touch with him.

A plaintive whinny split the air and Erin placed a comforting hand on the mare's belly.

"Not much longer now," she whispered, hoping it was the truth.

As the minutes ticked by, helplessness and frustration battled for control of Erin's emotions, swept along on a tide of "what ifs." What if she'd become a veterinarian instead of taking over the café from her mother? What if she hadn't chosen duty to her family over her dreams?

Then she would be able to offer something more than simple comfort or encouraging words as Diamond struggled to bring her foal into the world.

A ribbon of wind unfurled through the barn, carrying the sweet scent of pine and new-fallen snow. Erin's knees went weak with relief when she heard the soft tread of footsteps coming closer.

The stall door slid open behind her.

"Thank goodness you're here, Tweed," Erin said without turning around. "She's in a lot of pain but nothing seems to be happening."

Instead of a response marked by a crisp British accent, something the veterinarian wore as proudly as he did the tweed cap that had earned him his nickname, there was silence.

Erin shifted her weight and glanced over her shoulder. Her gaze locked on a pair of snow-covered hiking boots and traveled up. Over long legs encased in faded jeans. A flannel lined jacket. Broad shoulders. Sun-streaked blond hair. Chiseled features that formed the perfect setting for a pair of denim-blue eyes.

Lucas Clayton's eyes.

Lucas blinked several times, but the young woman kneeling in the straw didn't disappear.

And she looked just as shocked to see him.

The years melted away, burning through the layers of defenses Lucas had built up until all that remained were memories.

Memories of the one person who'd never stopped believing in him at a time in his life when Lucas had stopped believing in everything.

When Tweed had sent him on an emergency call, Lucas had only been given the address—not the name—of the person who needed help with a pregnant mare.

Erin Fields's unexpected presence not only stirred up emotions Lucas had buried long ago, but also created a few new ones.

The image frozen in his mind had been that of an eighteen-year-old girl. This Erin looked the same… but different.

The knee-length corduroy coat didn't quite conceal her willowy frame, but the sprinkle of ginger-colored freckles he'd often teased her about had faded. Windswept tendrils of copper hair framed features that had matured from a wholesome prettiness into a delicate, heart-stopping beauty.

He knew Erin hadn't left Clayton, but she wasn't supposed to be *here*. Inside an old barn adjacent to a dilapidated farmhouse a few miles outside of town. They'd both grown up in Clayton—their houses only a few blocks apart.

The mare tossed her head after sensing an unfamiliar presence, reminding Lucas why he was there.

Focus, buddy. In a town the size of Clayton, you knew you would see Erin sooner or later, he told himself.

Later would have been better.

The expression on Erin's face told him that she felt the same way.

"What are *you* doing here? Where's Tweed?"

"He had another call." Without waiting for an invitation, Lucas stepped into the stall. Kneeling down next to Erin, he caught a whiff of her shampoo, a light floral scent that reminded him of mountain lilies.

A scent that had no business lingering in his memory.

"I don't understand. Why would Tweed send you?" Erin shifted, putting a few more inches of space between them.

"He hired me." Lucas ran a hand over the horse's neck and felt the muscles ripple under the velvety skin.

"Hired…" Her gaze dropped to the medical kit he'd set down in the straw.

Lucas watched the myriad emotions topple like dominoes in a pair of eyes the color of warm gingerbread. Confusion. Disbelief. Denial.

"I'm here to help," Lucas said curtly. Being this close to Erin had opened a floodgate to his past and it was his way of trying to put a cap on the memories flooding in. "But if you'd rather wait for Tweed—"

"*No.* I just wasn't…" Erin averted her gaze. "Go ahead and do whatever you need to do."

Lucas opened the med kit and began to prep for an exam. "She belongs to you?"

Erin nodded. "I didn't realize Diamond was pregnant when I rescued her from the auction."

Diamond. It figured. Only Erin Fields would see

potential in an animal as battered and broken as this one. The number of scars crisscrossing the washboard ribs hinted at invisible ones below the surface.

Lucas worked quickly, aware that the woman beside him was watching every movement. He tried to keep his expression neutral, but she must have seen something there. Erin had always been good at reading him. Sometimes too good.

She leaned forward. "How is she?"

"In distress." Diamond's ears twitched at the sound of his voice, but she didn't even bother to lift her head. Lucas silently weighed his options.

"What can I do?"

"Keep her calm."

Erin had always been good at that, too. How many times had she listened to him as he vented about his mother's unreasonable expectations for his future plans? Taken his hand to absorb his volatile emotions, her lips moving in a silent prayer on his behalf? Been there for him without asking for anything in return?

Don't leave like this...

Lucas ruthlessly shook off the memory of the last night they'd spoken. A hundred miles down the road he'd realized that Erin had done the right thing when she'd refused to run away with him. He hadn't been fit to be a good husband back then.

Any more than he was fit to be a father now.

He turned to reach for a syringe only to find that Erin had anticipated his need. Their fingers brushed together and Lucas couldn't help but notice she wasn't wearing a ring. The realization that Erin wasn't married sent equal measures of relief and terror skittering through him.

"Talk to her." Lucas's voice came out sharper than he'd intended. "She's not going to like this."

Erin scooted closer to the horse and spoke to her in the same gentle, soothing voice she'd once used on him.

Lucas worked in silence for the next few minutes, administering a sedative to relax the horse while he performed a brief but enlightening internal exam.

He stood up after it was over and tried to ignore the pain that rattled down his spine, a subtle but persistent reminder of a conversation he'd had with a cranky bull the year before.

Erin looked up at him. "The foal is breech, isn't it?"

Lucas didn't miss the catch in her voice and he gave a curt nod, mentally bracing himself for the inevitable—telling her there was a good chance she would lose both the mare *and* the foal.

Lucas took a step toward her, shrinking the space between them. He could see the faint spray of ginger-colored freckles on her nose. The eyelashes spiked with unshed tears.

Something twisted in his gut. His sigh came out in a puff of frost. "Erin—"

"Don't say it," she said fiercely.

"You might have to choose," Lucas pushed.

"All right." Erin's chin lifted, warning him that she was willing to push back. "I choose both."

Lucas stared at her in disbelief. The girl he'd known in high school hadn't been a fighter. It was one of the things Lucas had accused her of the night he'd asked her to run away with him.

"When it comes right down to it, you're a coward, Erin. Your problem is that you have all these plans, all these big dreams, but you aren't willing to fight for them."

"And your problem is that you want to fight everything and everybody," Erin had said, her voice cracking under the weight of his accusation. *"You think if you leave Clayton, you'll leave behind your grief and all the regrets over your relationship with your dad—"*

"Don't bring my dad into this."

"Why not? You do it all the time. Every minute of every day. But if you leave Clayton like this, it's all going to follow you until you give it to God—"

"Leave Him out of it, too."

"Oh, Lucas..."

"Lucas?" Erin stood up. The top of her head was level with his shoulder but she didn't back down. "I'll help. Just tell me what I need to do."

"Leave." He didn't want her to witness what might happen. Or see him fail.

"Give me something else to do."

Was that a glimmer of humor in her eyes? Lucas

couldn't be sure but the warmth of it momentarily chased the chill away, if not the doubts.

"Diamond is strong," Erin whispered. "She's going to get through this."

There was a time when Erin had believed the same thing about him.

Before he'd walked away.

Erin tried to keep her thoughts centered on delivering the foal and her eyes off Lucas.

He worked with a calm efficiency that astonished her. As a teenager, Lucas had reminded Erin of a caged mountain lion. Filled with restless energy. Eyes fixed on some point in the horizon that no one else could see.

She didn't know this man. The one with the patient hands and soothing voice. It had taken Diamond several months to trust Erin enough to accept a treat from her hand, but in the space of five minutes Lucas had gained the mare's trust.

She still couldn't believe that he'd gone to college. Become a veterinarian.

Her dream…

"Erin?" Lucas's voice tugged at her.

She realized he'd caught her staring and blushed. "Sorry. What did you say?"

"The foal turned." In spite of the temperature outside, beads of sweat dotted Lucas's forehead. "I think we can let Mom take it from here."

Five minutes later, Diamond delivered a tiny, jet-black replica of herself.

Erin closed her eyes.

"Thank you, God," she murmured.

When she opened them again, she found Lucas staring at her, a wry expression on his face.

"Are you going to send Him the bill, too?"

Erin couldn't prevent a smile. And to her absolute amazement, Lucas smiled back. A faint quirk of his lips that carved out the dimple in his left cheek, a trait passed on from Clayton to Clayton like a family legacy.

Lucas hated it. Erin, however, had referred to it as the "Clayton brand" and teased him about it.

Pressed her lips against it.

Swallowing hard, she turned her attention to Diamond, severing the fragile connection that had sprung up between them. "There's a bucket of water and a clean towel in the tack room if you want to wash up."

"Thanks." The smile had disappeared.

Two polite strangers. That's what the years of silence had accomplished.

It's what Lucas had wanted, Erin reminded herself.

Diamond's soft whicker was a welcome distraction. The mare was nuzzling her newborn foal, who lifted its head in response to the attention.

Caught up in the wonder of the moment, Erin

watched the two interact until Lucas returned and began to collect his medical supplies.

"Everything looks good but I'd keep a close eye on her for the next twenty-four hours." He turned to her, his gaze once again distant. "I'll give you my cell number in case there's a problem."

Erin caught her lower lip between her teeth. She didn't want his phone number. Didn't want to see him again and deal with the stampede of emotions those denim-blue eyes triggered.

"That's not necessary. I'll call Tweed if I have any questions. He's treated Diamond since I brought her home."

"Tweed…" Lucas hesitated. "He's planning to retire around the first of the year. Until then, he wants to stay in the clinic and limit his practice to pets."

Erin sucked in a breath, hoping that didn't mean what she thought it meant.

"I'm taking over the large animal side of his practice."

That's what she'd thought it meant.

"You're staying in Clayton?" Erin tried to keep her voice steady.

"It looks that way. For a year." Lucas didn't sound happy about it, either.

So the rumors she'd heard about George Sr.'s will had been true. Until now, she hadn't quite believed it.

"Yoo-hoo! Is anyone home?" A feminine voice floated through the barn.

"We're in here," Lucas called back.

A few seconds later, Mei Clayton appeared in the doorway, holding the hand of an adorable preschool-age boy. A bright red snowsuit enveloped his thin frame but instead of a stocking cap, a cowboy hat was perched on his head. A battered black Stetson that looked a lot like the one Lucas used to wear.

He smiled shyly, pressed his cheek against Mei's leg and pointed to the foal. "Thatsa baby horse."

Erin couldn't help but smile back. "Babysitting today?"

Lucas and Mei exchanged a look that Erin couldn't decipher.

"This is Max," Mei said.

"Hey, Max." Erin experienced the familiar pang that happened whenever a cute little kid came into the café. *Someday.* "I'm Erin. It's nice to meet you. Do you like horses?"

"I like trucks better," Max declared.

Erin winked at Mei. "We'll have to work on that."

"What's up, sis?" Lucas shrugged his coat on. His sister slanted an apologetic look in his direction.

"I know I promised to watch Max this afternoon, but the high-school secretary called and asked if I would be available to attend an emergency parent-teacher conference after school. You didn't answer your cell so I called Tweed to track you down."

"That's okay." The affectionate smile Lucas gave

her told Erin the siblings still shared a close bond. "I'm finished here."

Max broke away from Mei. And to Erin's astonishment, he headed straight for Lucas.

Her gaze bounced from Lucas's sister to the boy, who'd wrapped both arms around Lucas's knees and was clinging to him like a burr on a wool sock.

Lucas looked so uncomfortable with the attention that Erin had to stifle a smile.

"So, who does this little cowboy belong to?" She directed the question at Mei but it was Lucas who answered.

"He belongs to me."

Chapter Three

Lucas saw the flash of hurt in Erin's eyes before she could disguise it.

"I see," she murmured.

Lucas doubted that. How could she? Even he wasn't sure how he'd ended up with custody of someone else's child.

He could almost guess what she was thinking. He was the guy who avoided family obligations like a disease. Sure, he'd been willing to marry Erin, but Lucas had come to realize that the proposal had been offered out of selfishness. He'd claimed he didn't want to lose her, but what he hadn't wanted to lose was the sense of peace she had brought to his life.

Which made him *that* guy.

The guy who had no business taking on the responsibility of a wife. Or a child.

"Oh, before I forget, here's the Realtor's number." Mei fished a business card out of her coat pocket and handed it to him. "I ran into Bev yesterday afternoon and mentioned that you're anxious to find something."

Anxious to move out of his childhood home, Lucas thought. The last few days hadn't been easy. Mei had done her best to ease the tension between him and their mother, but Lisette made no attempt to hide her disappointment in him. Something Lucas should have been used to by now.

Not only did his mother barely interact with Max, she'd refused to care for him when Lucas went out on a call. Mei babysat when she was available, but Lucas knew he couldn't count on her generosity much longer. When his sister wasn't substitute teaching at the high school, she was spending time with Jack McCord, the local search-and-rescue worker who had crossed state lines to bring him and Max to safety.

Lucas still couldn't wrap his mind around that relationship. Mei and Jack, Charley Clayton's stepson, had been at odds in high school but now they claimed to be in love. There seemed to be a lot of that going around, now that he thought about it.

So he wasn't going to think about it.

"Thanks, Mei. I'll try to give her a call after Max goes to bed tonight."

Max frowned. "Don't wanna go to bed."

"You have to learn to spell things," Mei whispered to Lucas.

"Spell things?"

"You know. B-e-d." Mei closed one eye in a saucy wink and blew Max a kiss before breezing out the door. "Bye, partner. Bye, Erin."

"Bye." Erin's smile, when aimed at his sister, was relaxed and genuine.

Lucas couldn't help but feel a little envious.

There'd been a time when they were completely at ease in each other's company. Now, she could barely look at him.

"I'll drop a check off tomorrow." Erin's gaze drifted to Max again.

"No hurry—" Lucas found himself talking to her back. He took Max by the hand and followed Erin out of the barn. "I'll swing by in a few days to check on Diamond. Is there someone around here during the day?"

"I'm usually at the café." Erin veered toward the shoveled pathway leading to the house.

"I know that, but the owners won't mind if I stop by, right?"

She whirled around and sent a spray of snow over the tops of his boots. "What do you mean, the owners?"

Now it was his turn to be confused. "The people who board Diamond for you."

"I don't board her here. I *live* here."

Frowning, Lucas peered at the two-story eyesore with the dingy white clapboard siding, crooked shutters and a wraparound porch that sagged like an unbuckled belt around its middle. The small outbuildings and barn were in a similar state of disrepair.

"What happened to your house in town?"

Erin looked away. "I sold it after Mom died."

Lucas felt his stomach turn inside out. Erin's mother had battled diabetes for years, but no one had bothered to mention that she'd passed away. When had it happened? And why had Erin stayed in Clayton?

She'd been as anxious as he was to leave their hometown, her goal to become a large animal vet. Lucas's goal had been to break every household rule his parents established.

Did Erin realize she had been instrumental in his choice of a career? Every retired, broken-down ranch horse within a twenty-five mile radius of Clayton had received her loving attention and he'd been right there beside her, currycomb in hand.

His willingness to work with the animals had caught the attention of the local vet on the ranch he'd worked in Georgia.

"You have a way with these critters, Clayton," the doc had said. *"Ever think of making a living at it?"*

Until that moment, Lucas hadn't. But he'd taken the words to heart—and didn't mention that his "way with critters" had been encouraged by a slender girl with big brown eyes and a luminous smile.

He pulled his thoughts back in line. Looking back had the power to make a man stumble.

"I'm sorry." The words sounded inadequate but they were the best Lucas could do.

"So am I," Erin said softly.

"So you bought a..." Lucas searched for the right word. One that wouldn't offend her. "A...house... out here."

A shadow of a smile touched Erin's lips. She'd read his mind. Again. "I'm planning to fix up the place a little at a time and add a few more stalls so I can rescue more horses like Diamond. I think the place has potential."

Lucas didn't have the heart to tell her that she was wrong. The same way she'd been wrong about him.

"I can help. I gottsa hammer," Max announced.

"Really?" Erin reached out and tapped a finger against the tip of his wind-kissed button nose. "You'll have to show it to me sometime."

Max looked troubled and Lucas knew what was coming next.

Sure enough, tears welled up in the hazel eyes. "Hammer's at home."

And home, no matter how rough it had been, was a place that existed only in Max's memory now.

A familiar feeling of helplessness once again threatened to swamp Lucas, reminding him that he was in way over his head. He didn't know what to do about the fresh pain in Max's eyes...or the shadows that still lingered in Erin's from the loss of her mother.

Maybe because he'd never figured out how to deal with his own grief.

Losing his father in the car accident that had also claimed the life of his uncle, George Jr., had changed him. Outwardly, no one could see the damage. On the inside, it was a different story. Like tempered glass, Lucas absorbed the impact of the blow but hadn't been able to stop the tiny cracks from spreading below the surface. Sometimes he felt as if they'd changed the very structure of his soul.

"Wanna go home," Max choked out.

"We're setting up camp together, remember? You'll have your own room and a shelf full of toys."

It was bribery, plain and simple. The parenting books would disapprove, but it was the best Lucas could do.

Glancing at Erin, he braced himself for the reproach he probably deserved.

The compassion in the golden-brown eyes rocked him to the core.

"You're looking for a place of your own?" she ventured.

"Mom isn't used to little kids in the house anymore." Especially a little kid who woke up in the night, caught in the throes of a waking nightmare.

"There's a place just down the road for sale," Erin said, almost reluctantly. "The couple who lives there wants to relocate to Florida to be closer to their daughter."

Lucas didn't bother to tell her that he was interested in a house he could rent, not buy. Buying a house meant putting down roots and he was only in Clayton for a year. He silently corrected himself. *Eleven months and three weeks.*

"I didn't notice a For Sale sign on the way here."

"There isn't one yet." Erin pushed her hands into her coat pockets. "I heard it's going on the market this weekend."

The only place Lucas remembered seeing was a log cabin set back from the road a ways. Small and cozy and surrounded by a yard large enough to appeal to an active boy.

But way too close to Erin.

Seven years ago she'd been both confidante and conscience. His best friend and his first love.

After the way they'd parted, Lucas wasn't sure what they were anymore. But there was one thing he did know.

The thought of staying in Clayton for a year wasn't nearly as terrifying as the thought of being Erin Fields's closest neighbor.

"How long does it take for a guy to get a cup of coffee around this place?"

Erin's back teeth ground together.

Vincent Clayton had sauntered in five minutes before closing time, leaving a trail of mud and slush across her freshly mopped floor before taking a seat at the farthest table from the kitchen.

He loved to do that.

Erin found herself wishing that she hadn't sent Gerald and Jerome Hicks home early. Business had been slow so she'd convinced the two cooks that she could handle any last-minute customers and shooed them out the door.

Help me be patient, Lord. Erin sent up the silent prayer as she made her way to Vincent's table. He smiled at her, his casual pose as deceptive as that of a rattlesnake coiled up in the sun.

She didn't trust him for a second. This particular snake was always ready—and willing—to strike.

Erin suppressed a shudder as she filled his coffee cup. "Sorry for the delay," she said automatically. "I had to put on a fresh pot."

Instead of looking at the menu, Vincent's gaze swept around the empty dining room. "I guess it's just you and me, isn't it, Red?"

"What would you like?"

The sudden glint in the shifty blue eyes made Erin regret the way she'd worded the question. "Now that's an interesting question," he drawled. "Could be that I want the same thing my cousin wants."

"Leave Zach and Kylie alone," Erin warned. "They're happy."

"Who said I was talking about Zach?"

Erin sensed the rage simmering just below the

surface of his smile and knew if she followed it to its source, it would lead her to the one family member who had always been Vincent's greatest rival.

Lucas.

It was hard to believe the two men were related. They didn't resemble each other in looks or personality. Whereas Lucas had frequently been blamed for his role in things he'd never even taken part in, his cousin had somehow managed to come out smelling like the proverbial rose.

Even now, Vincent had no qualms about using his father Pauley's title as part-time mayor to throw his weight around.

"It's late. What would you like to order?" Erin somehow managed to keep her voice steady.

"I heard he brought a kid back with him. Wonder how long that'll last?" Vincent leaned back, hooking the heels of his snow-covered boots over the rung of the wooden chair beneath the table.

Erin stiffened. "I imagine it will last awhile. Max *is* his son."

"His son?" Vincent hooted. "That kid ain't got a drop of Clayton blood in his veins. Lucas took him in like a stray pup after the boy's daddy died."

Erin fought to hide her reaction.

When Lucas had said that Max belonged to him, Erin had searched for a resemblance between the two, some trait passed on from father to son, but had come to the conclusion that the boy must favor his mother.

Vincent's claim would explain why Lucas had looked so uncomfortable when Max had clung to him in her barn that day.

Bits and pieces of rumors that Erin had heard over the past few months began to fall into place.

The sudden silences and worried looks she'd seen pass between the Clayton family had led her to believe that Lucas was refusing to come back and fulfill the terms of his grandfather's will.

Now she wondered if the delay hadn't had something to do with Max.

"Lucas says he's going to legally adopt the kid, but that won't happen," Vincent went on. "We both know that Lucas was never what you'd call a 'family man.'"

Erin had had her fill of the man's poison. "He came back, didn't he?"

The triumphant look in Vincent's eyes told her that she'd made a mistake. It didn't matter if he'd been bluffing or if he had somehow known about her and Lucas all along. She'd stuck up for Lucas—the way she always had. If Vincent's plan was to force Erin into admitting that her feelings for Lucas hadn't changed, she'd just delivered the answer. Gift-wrapped and ready to use against her.

"But he won't stay long." Vincent shook his head in mock sympathy. "Not for old man Clayton's money or his land. Lucas ain't wired that way and everybody with a lick of sense knows it."

His tone implied that Erin Fields didn't fall into the "people with a lick of sense" category.

"If you don't want anything, I'm going to close up for the night."

Vincent's hand shot out, his fingers curling around her wrist. "I want what's mine and Lucas isn't going to cheat me out of it."

Erin and Vincent might have played in the same sandbox once upon a time, but that didn't prevent her knees from locking up in fear as the pressure tightened.

She sucked in a breath. "Let go."

Vincent released her and sprang to his feet. "Mark my words. A lot can happen in a year." The gleam in his eyes was more intimidating than the grip of his hand had been. "He won't stick it out."

"People change."

"Some do…and some don't." Vincent leaned in close, enveloping her in a cloud of pungent cologne. "If I were you, I wouldn't be getting any ideas about a happily-ever-after with my cousin. You weren't enough to make Lucas stay back then, Erin, and you won't be enough for him now."

He sauntered to the door and the moment it snapped shut behind him, Erin was there, fumbling with the lock. She squeezed her eyes shut and pressed her forehead against the frosted glass.

Her heart had instantly rejected Vincent's claim

that Lucas planned to leave Max with someone else. Yes, he'd appeared uncomfortable with the way the preschooler had clung to him, but she hadn't missed Lucas's awkward but tender attempt to comfort him, either.

No matter what Vincent said, Lucas cared about Max.

But unfortunately, Erin knew what Vincent had said about her *was* true.

She was still the same woman she'd been seven years ago.

The woman that Lucas had left.

Chapter Four

"We goin' to Erin's house?"

In the rearview mirror, Lucas saw Max point out the window. The wide smile on the boy's face hadn't been there a few seconds ago.

Max must have met half the population of Clayton since their arrival. The fact that he remembered Erin's name proved she'd made an impression.

Maybe it hadn't been such a good idea to bring him along.

An overweight corgi rounded the barn, sounding an alarm as his pickup rolled down the snow-packed driveway.

A moment later, Erin stepped out of the building, her copper hair a bright spot of color against the faded timber siding.

Lucas's heart stumbled at the sight of her.

There had always been *something* about Erin Fields. Some elusive quality that went beyond simple chemistry or the way she looked—although she was more beautiful at twenty-five than she'd been at eighteen.

When Lucas returned to Clayton, he knew it would be awkward to see Erin again. Even though they'd parted in anger the night he left, they had a history. Shared memories. The trouble was, Lucas hadn't been prepared for the emotions tangled inside of those memories.

Erin was a complication he didn't need. He'd left Clayton once, and after he fulfilled the terms of his grandfather's will he planned to leave it again.

"Wanna get out, Lucas!" Max tugged on the strap of his booster seat.

"Hold on." Lucas hopped out of the truck cab and opened the door.

Giggling, Max made a break for it as soon as Lucas unbuckled him. The kid was smart enough to know where to seek sanctuary, too. He made a beeline for Erin, who swung Max up in her arms as if she'd done it a hundred times before and tucked him against the curve of her hip.

"How are you doing today, cowboy?"

"I wanna see the baby horse." Max pointed to the barn.

"She's with her momma right now," Erin said. "And they're both doing great."

Lucas figured that last bit was meant for him.

"Max and I had a few errands to run this morning so I thought I'd stop by." He hadn't called to let Erin know that he was on his way over. In fact, he'd planned the morning visit because she'd told him the majority of her time was spent at the café. Apparently, however, that didn't mean today.

As he followed her into the barn, Max chattered on about the "black-and-blue" pancakes Lucas had made for breakfast.

"Cowboys like 'em the best," he told her matter-of-factly.

"Really? I didn't know that." Erin glanced at Lucas. "How do you make, ah, black-and-blue pancakes?"

"It's easy," he said ruefully. "The blue comes from the blueberries and the black when you forget to flip them while you're stirring the orange juice."

Erin's laughter swept through the barn...and his defenses. Lucas found it difficult to take his eyes off her.

Not a good sign.

Erin put a finger to her lips before sliding open the stall door. "Shh. Diamond likes it quiet so her baby can sleep."

"I'll be quiet," Max promised, staring up at Erin as if she were a fairy-tale princess come to life. A fairy-tale princess in faded corduroy and denim.

She looked totally at peace in her surroundings, something Lucas had never quite managed to achieve.

Maybe because it didn't seem to matter that he'd juggled classes and work during the day and studied long into the night to earn his degree in veterinary

science, graduating a year earlier than his class-
mates. No matter how much Lucas accomplished,
he always heard his father's voice tell him it wasn't
enough.

*"You have a rebellious nature, Lucas. If you don't
listen to me and do what I say, you're never going
to amount to anything. You'll disappoint everyone
who cares about you and you'll be alone. Sometimes
I think that's what you want."*

The words had cut deep, embedding themselves
in Lucas's heart. He'd discovered that nothing, not
a steady paycheck, not pats on the back nor praise
from his boss, could erase the words his father had
spoken to him on the night he'd died.

They'd taken root and grown. Crowded out his
ability to commit until he'd become the man Vern
Clayton had predicted he would be.

*"God loves you, Lucas, and He won't turn His
back on you. You'll never be alone."*

Erin's voice sounded sweet and clear, as if she'd
just spoken the words out loud instead of years ago.

What would his life be like if he'd believed her,
not his father?

Something shifted inside of Lucas and he struggled to regain his balance. "If you have something
to do, go ahead," he said curtly. "Max and I won't
be here long."

That was one promise Lucas would make sure he
kept.

"That's all right." The wary look in Erin's eyes

had returned. "I'll introduce Max to Butterscotch and her kittens while you check on Diamond."

Because she didn't want to spend any more time in his company than necessary.

Lucas should have felt the same way. So why did he have the overwhelming urge to follow Erin as she led Max away?

Diamond greeted him with a snort as he stepped into the stall.

"Yeah, I know," Lucas muttered. "The sooner we get this over with, the sooner our lives can get back to normal."

As normal as life in Clayton would ever get, Lucas silently amended. And with Erin Fields less than fifty feet away, she was out of sight but definitely not out of mind.

The music of her laughter echoed through the barn and Lucas paused to listen until Diamond swung her head around and nipped his sleeve.

He was definitely out of his mind.

Ten minutes later Lucas found Erin and Max in a corner of the barn, playing with a litter of half-grown calico kittens with lime-green eyes. Max ambled over and tugged on his arm until Lucas bent down.

"Haveta go, Lucas," he whispered.

"We will, buddy. As soon as I put my things away."

"No." Max shook his head vigorously. "Haveta *go*."

Oh, *that* kind of go.

Lucas silently calculated how long it would take to get the nearest gas station without exceeding the speed limit. "Five minutes, Bud."

"But I haveta go *now*."

Erin sighed. "I do have indoor plumbing, Lucas."

"Are you sure?"

Erin didn't bother to grace that with a response, just closed the barn door and strode toward the house. They followed her inside, where the scent of cinnamon and apples permeated the air.

She pointed to a door at the end of the narrow hall. "Come into the kitchen when you're done. I have to take a loaf of bread out of the oven."

Lucas scooped Max up to hasten the trip but as they passed the living room, the boy let out a squeal that practically drilled a hole in Lucas's left eardrum.

"Look at Erin's tree!"

Lucas blinked. It wasn't just a tree. The entire room resembled a Christmas card come to life.

The roundest balsam fir Lucas had ever seen took up an entire corner of the room, decked out in dozens of shimmering ornaments that caught and reflected the twinkling lights woven between the branches. A pine garland braided with gold ribbons ran the length of the fireplace mantle and a hand-carved nativity set graced the coffee table in front of the green corduroy sofa.

Lucas wanted to smack himself upside the head. Christmas was only three weeks away and until now it hadn't even appeared on his radar. His mother hadn't decorated for the holiday. Maybe she didn't bother anymore. But after what Max had been through…well, he deserved some of this.

The scents and sounds of the holiday.

A home.

Unfortunately, Lucas didn't feel equipped to give the boy either one of them.

Erin appeared beside him. "I decorate the house the day after Thanksgiving every year. It's a tradition Mom started."

"I remember," Lucas said without thinking.

Erin's lips parted but no words came out. Maybe because there wasn't anything to say that would banish the memories that crowded the air whenever they were together.

Max broke the silence. "What's that?" He pointed at the nativity set, but Lucas shook his head.

"Sorry, buddy. First things first."

Fortunately, Max accepted Lucas's decision without a fuss, but there was no stopping him from taking a detour into the living room on their way back. Erin must have known that because she was waiting for them in the hallway.

"Do you mind?" Lucas needed permission before turning a four-year-old boy loose into her Christmas wonderland.

Erin shook her head. "There isn't anything he can damage."

"I'm not so sure about that," Lucas muttered. As

well behaved as Max was, he'd managed to turn Lisette's home upside down in the space of a week. Fingerprints on the walls. A broken dish. Plastic trucks making roads in her potted plants.

Lucas had heard about it all. Which was why they had to find a place of their own. Soon.

His cell phone rang and he glanced at the name on the screen. "It's Tweed," he murmured, keeping a watchful eye on Max. "I should probably take it."

Erin nodded. "Come on, Max. I have a special ornament on the tree. Let's see if you can find it." She took the boy by the hand and led him into the living room.

By the time Lucas returned, he found Max snuggled up on Erin's lap, one of the nativity pieces clutched in his hand.

"Is everything all right?" Erin asked.

"One of Fred McKinney's steers sliced its leg open and he thinks it's going to need stitches."

"What about Max?" Erin frowned. "Is he going with you?"

Lucas didn't get a chance to answer because Max sat up straight and began to shake his head.

"Nope. I'm stayin' with Erin."

"Listen, buddy—"

"Bye, Lucas. See ya later." Max flashed an enchanting smile that Erin matched with one of her own.

"I guess he's staying with me."

Lucas wondered if the preschooler wasn't smarter

than he was. Because looking at Erin, at the warm light in her eyes and the arms wrapped protectively around his adopted son, he was suddenly having a hard time remembering why he'd ever left.

Erin ran a damp dishcloth over the refrigerator door and erased another smudge of green frosting.

The table resembled an artist's palette and flour dusted the floor, making it look as if her kitchen had been the target of an early snow. By the time Erin pulled the last batch of cookies out of the oven, Max had been coated in a thin layer of frosting and sprinkles, looking a bit like one of the gingerbread men lining the counter.

She couldn't help but smile at the memory.

Max was one hundred percent boy. Bright. Energetic. Inquisitive. And heartbreakingly sweet.

The trouble was, Erin had already had her heart broken once.

She turned the handle of the faucet with a little more force than was necessary.

Maybe she shouldn't have been so quick to agree to babysit.

But somehow, Max's wide, little boy grin had pushed every one of her doubts about keeping her distance from Lucas aside.

She padded down the hallway to the living room, where she'd left Max playing with the nativity set while she straightened up the kitchen. The wooden figurines had fascinated him. Erin had answered a dozen questions about each piece and tried to explain, in a way that a four year old could understand, why there was a baby sleeping inside the miniature barn.

Max's lack of knowledge about the Christmas story made her heart ache.

As the son of a medical missionary, Lucas knew the Bible inside and out, but he had turned his back on his faith when they were in high school. He'd told Erin that he probably wouldn't be able to live up to God's expectations any more than he could his father's, so why even try?

And even though Lucas had walked away from her, too, Erin had never stopped praying that he would eventually find his way back to God. Over the past few days, she'd felt the burden to pray for him even more.

There's a reason You brought Lucas back to Clayton, Lord. Show him that You love him and help him let go of the past. Max needs Lucas to be a loving father...and Lucas needs You to show him how.

Peeking around the corner, she spotted the boy curled up on the sofa next to Winston, sound asleep, the ragged tail of his blanket clutched in one small hand.

An image of Lucas, holding the rumpled square of bright green fleece, rose up in her mind. He'd retrieved the blanket from the truck and brought it up to the house to give to Max before he'd left. Erin had been touched by the gesture, but the self-conscious look on Lucas's face told her that he wasn't comfortable with his new role.

Erin wasn't completely comfortable with it, either.

He belongs to me.

Lucas. A father.

How many hours had she spent doodling their names in her notebook during study hall? Planning their wedding? Their family?

Their *future.*

Until he'd set out on his own and crushed every one of those girlish fantasies. Erin's faith had been the only thing holding her together during those first few days. And as those days turned into months and the months became years, new dreams eventually began to kindle from the ashes of the ones that had once revolved around Lucas.

If you keep looking back, you might miss something good that's right there in front of you.

One of her mom's many pearls of wisdom. And one that Erin had finally taken to heart. It was the reason she kept a smile on her face and her calendar full. Every morning she asked God to teach her contentment—to show her the good that was right in front of her.

And right now, no matter how conflicted her feelings for Lucas Clayton might be, the "good" in front of her was Max.

As Erin leaned down to tuck a corner of the blanket more snuggly around his thin shoulders, she heard a soft knock on the front door.

By the time she reached the doorframe, Lucas already stood in the front hallway. And once again, her traitorous heart stalled at the sight of him.

Lucas had always been good-looking, but the last seven years had wrought subtle changes. At six foot two, he still towered above her, but he was no longer the lanky teenager that Erin remembered. The sun had permanently stained his skin a golden-bronze, a striking contrast to those incredible blue eyes. *Clayton blue,* Erin had heard someone call them once.

Erin remembered Lucas rolling his eyes when she'd repeated the comment.

"First we get a town named after us and now a color. What's next? A mountain range? A national monument?"

"There's nothing wrong with the name Clayton." Erin had given him a playful swat on the arm.

Lucas had smiled that slow smile that never failed to melt her heart like butter in a hot skillet. *"I'm glad you feel that way."*

Erin had been afraid to read too much into the statement. Until Lucas had leaned forward and kissed her.

Her first kiss…

Don't. Look. Back.

Erin silently repeated the words. Lucas Clayton happened to be part of her past and, thanks to George Sr.'s will, an unexpected part of her present. But he was definitely *not* a part of her future.

That's what she needed to remember.

"Lucas." She flashed a polite smile—the same one that every cowboy who came into the café received with a cup of coffee.

He drove a hand through his hair and snowflakes drifted down like bits of silver confetti. "I'm sorry it's so late. Is Max ready to leave?"

"He's sound asleep."

"Right." Lucas sighed. "He usually takes a nap around this time. I'll carry him out to the truck."

Something in the weary slump of his shoulders tugged at her conscience.

"Would you like to thaw out with a cup of coffee first?" Erin couldn't believe she'd said the words. Out loud.

And Lucas hesitated just long enough to make her wish she could take back the invitation.

Chapter Five

"Sure." The husky rumble of Lucas's voice scraped away another layer from her defenses. "I appreciate it."

No problem.

Erin wanted to say the words but they got stuck in her throat. She was all too aware of Lucas as he followed her into the kitchen.

He let out a low whistle. "Max must have slept a long time."

"What makes you say that?"

One eyebrow lifted. "The ten dozen Christmas cookies on your counter?"

"It's only five dozen." Erin reached for a clean coffee mug in the dish drainer. "And Max wasn't sleeping. He helped me."

"Max *helped* you?" Lucas repeated in disbelief.

"Technically, we divided the work. I baked the cookies and Max decorated them."

Lucas's lips twitched. "I guess the three-eyed snowmen should have given it away."

Erin filled the mug, trying to keep her wits about her. Which wasn't easy with Lucas three feet away. Close enough for her to breathe in the scent of leather, crisp mountain air and the hint of soap that was uniquely his.

You can do this. Just pretend you're at the café and he's a customer, remember? "Do you take cream or sugar?"

"Just black."

So far, so good. "How did it go out at the Mc-Kinney place?"

Instead of taking a drink, Lucas folded his hands around the steaming mug, as if trying to absorb its warmth. "Ten stitches."

"Ouch." Erin winced.

"Don't feel too bad for the steer," Lucas said drily. "He only ended up with six of them."

"Then who…" For the first time, Erin noticed the gauze bandage peeking out from the cuff of Lucas's sleeve. "*You* got the other four?"

"That's why I'm late. Arabella called my cell when I was on my way back and I happened to mention the injury. I'll know better next time. Jonathan Turner was waiting in the driveway when I got back to the clinic," Lucas said, his expression rueful. "I heard she was dating a doctor but I didn't think I'd meet the guy while he was stitching up my hand."

"What happened?" Erin was almost afraid to ask.

"Apparently he didn't like my bedside manner—the steer, not Mr. McKinney." Lucas shrugged. "It comes with the job, you know."

"I'll have to take your word for that."

An awkward silence filled the space between them. Was Lucas remembering how she'd once dreamed of being a veterinarian?

Their eyes met across the table and Lucas set the cup down.

"I should go. Thanks again for keeping an eye on Max."

Just like that.

Erin's throat tightened. Apparently Lucas found it no more difficult to walk away from her now than he had all those years ago. Further proof that his feelings hadn't been as deep as hers.

You weren't enough to keep him here...

Vincent's mocking words cycled through her mind and she turned away so Lucas wouldn't see her expression. In her heart of hearts, Erin might wish for Lucas to still feel *something* for her, but she didn't want it to be pity.

Poor Erin Fields. Still hung up on her first crush.

She needed to pray that God would help *her* let go of the past, too.

"I'll pack up some cookies for you to take home." Erin reached for a decorative tin on the second shelf and began to pack it with three-eyed snowmen and pink reindeer, hoping Lucas wouldn't notice that her hands were shaking.

Which wouldn't have been as obvious if he'd remained sitting at the table. But no. He got up, closed the distance between them in two short strides and began to help.

"You've got green and red sprinkles in your hair."

"Christmas decorations," Erin shot back, a little surprised that she could do polite *and* funny. "I get a little carried away."

Lucas, however, didn't appear amused. His eyes narrowed, searching her face as if he were looking for something. Or someone.

What did he see when he looked at her? The girl he'd claimed to have loved? Or one more mistake he'd made?

The air emptied out of Erin's lungs as his fingers brushed against her hair. "Erin—"

Whatever he'd been about to say was lost in the high-pitched scream that pierced the air.

Not again.

Not *now*.

Lucas sprinted down the hall, vaguely aware that Erin was right behind him, already apologizing for something he knew wasn't her fault.

He should have warned her this could happen, but he hadn't anticipated being gone so long. And the truth was, he never knew when a dark memory would emerge and trigger another one of Max's episodes.

The social worker had encouraged Lucas to give

Max time to adjust to all the changes in his life. He'd gone through a lot for someone of his tender age, but he didn't have the ability to process what had happened. Reality and imagination had a way of becoming tangled. The result was a waking nightmare for Max and a sleepless night for Lucas.

He rounded the corner and spotted Max bolt upright on the sofa, his small body rigid with terror, eyes wide and riveted on some unseen threat.

Erin's soft gasp punctuated the air and Lucas remembered how he'd felt the first time he'd seen Max like this. The way he *still* felt when he saw Max like this.

He glanced at Erin to gauge her reaction. To his astonishment, she didn't rush over, pick Max up and rattle off a bunch of questions that he couldn't answer. She stopped in the center of the room, as if she trusted that Lucas knew what to do.

Yeah, right.

When it came to stuff like this, Lucas would have loved to defer to an expert. Unfortunately, there was never one around when you needed one. Max was stuck with a guy who knew more about four-year-old horses than four-year-old boys.

He lowered himself onto the sofa next to Max as casually as if they were going to watch Monday-night football.

"Hey, buddy." Lucas didn't expect a response. He'd learned that words couldn't penetrate the invisible wall that separated them, but talking to Max made *him* feel better.

He slanted a quick look at Erin. She was watching them but her lips moved in a silent plea.

This was the second time he'd caught her praying. Erin's faith had been strong as a teenager and it looked as if she'd held on to it over the years.

That made one of them.

Lucas felt a stab of envy that a close relationship with God had always seemed to come so naturally to her. Over the past few months, when he'd tried to get Max to safety, there'd been times he had wanted to call on God but figured he no longer had the right. He'd made a decision a long time ago to make his own way—it seemed a little hypocritical to ask for help when things got tough. Still, it was comforting to think that God might intervene on Max's behalf because Erin was the one doing the asking.

Ignoring the dull ache from the stitches in his arm, Lucas carefully drew Max against his chest and waited. The only sound in the room came from the crackle and spit of the logs in the fireplace.

As if Max were a frozen statue coming back to life, Lucas gradually felt the thin shoulders relax. The rapid drumbeat of his heart began to even out.

"Lucas?" Max whimpered.

"I'm right here, buddy."

"It's dark."

The fireplace cast plenty of light, but Lucas didn't argue. He wasn't sure if Max had always been afraid of the dark or if it had something to do with the fact that when Lucas found him, he'd been locked in a windowless room not much bigger than a closet.

Erin moved across the room, and Lucas assumed she was going to turn on another light. Instead, she reached down and plugged in the Christmas tree. Hundreds of tiny lights, in a rainbow of colors, began to wink in the branches.

Max hooked two fingers in his cheek and settled against Lucas's shoulder, his gaze focused on the lights rather than the dark memory that had held him captive in its grip.

"Something sure smells good, Erin." Lucas sniffed the air appreciatively. "Like...cookies?"

Erin caught on immediately. "That's right. Gingerbread," she said, her light tone matching his.

Max looked up at him. "Me and Erin maked 'em."

Lucas felt the knot in his chest loosen. "I'll bet they're delicious."

"I ate a tree with sprinkles," Max informed him. "Erin eats the frostin' with a spoon."

"Is that so?" Lucas bit back a smile as color bloomed in Erin's cheeks.

"Someone has to taste test it." The concern in her eyes remained, but she reached out and playfully tweaked Max's toes. "You can take some cookies home for your grandma and Aunt Mei. How about that?"

"An' Jamie an' Julie an' Jessie?" Fear dissipated

like a morning mist, unveiling a familiar sparkle in Max's eyes.

"Ahh." Erin looked at him in understanding. "He met Arabella's triplets."

"Yesterday." Lucas winced at the memory.

For an entire week after his arrival, settling Max in and working out the details of his new job had been handy excuses to avoid his extended family.

He'd gotten good at dodging them until Mei cornered him in their mother's kitchen with a message from his cousin, Arabella Michaels. It was time he "make the rounds" and introduce Max to his new family.

Starting with her.

Lucas had braced himself for that first official reunion with a member of his extended family, anticipating anything from awkward silence to outright hostility that he'd returned to Clayton so close to the deadline.

Instead, Lucas had been shocked by the warm welcome he'd received. Something had changed in his family but he wasn't sure what it was. And probably wouldn't be around long enough to find out...

"They're sweet little girls," Erin was saying.

"They're trouble in triplicate," Lucas muttered. "They were playing 'wedding.' If I hadn't stepped in, they would have painted Max's fingernails pink."

Erin's lips curved into a smile. "I'm not surprised, with Jasmine and Cade's wedding coming up in a few weeks."

"Mei mentioned they were getting married on Christmas Eve."

She nodded. "Everyone has been chipping in to help. Kylie Jones has been acting as Jasmine's unofficial wedding planner, and Vivienne is planning the menu for the reception. Arabella is baking the cake and Zach is going to walk her down the aisle."

Lucas was stunned into silence—and not only because Erin knew more about what was going in his cousins' lives than he did.

"You don't approve?"

"I guess I'm surprised *they* do," he admitted. "Nothing against Jasmine or Cade, but they just graduated from high school last spring. They're pretty young to tie themselves down like that. They have their whole future ahead of them."

He saw Erin's expression change and wished he could take back the words.

But it was too late.

Jasmine and Cade weren't much older than they'd been the night Lucas had shown up at her door and proposed. No candlelight or flowers. Not even a ring.

Erin had deserved better than what he'd offered the night he left town.

She still did.

Erin tried not to let Lucas see how his comment had affected her.

If she'd ever wondered if he'd regretted leaving her behind, she didn't have to wonder anymore.

Once he'd crossed the Colorado state line, he'd probably turned a few cartwheels, relieved that he didn't have anyone "tying him down."

She turned her attention back to Max, who had been listening to their exchange with wide-eyed fascination, and tapped a finger against the tip of his nose. If Lucas could pretend everything was fine, so could she.

"How about I make sure you have enough cookies for the whole family?"

"Okay." Max reached for a wooden camel on the coffee table and held it up in front of Lucas. "This one's Bob."

"Bob, huh? That's a good name." Lucas kept a straight face as he examined the carving.

Erin watched the exchange, still not exactly sure what had happened.

When she'd heard Max scream, she assumed that he had rolled off the sofa in his sleep. But Lucas had brushed aside her apology, as if he'd known something else had happened.

Erin's stomach had dropped to her feet when she'd seen Max sitting on the sofa, the color stripped from his rosy cheeks and his pupils dilated with fear. She'd seen wounded animals in that condition but never a child.

But Lucas didn't appear shocked by the sight. He'd looked...resigned.

Because he'd gone through it before.

The thought struck her with the force of a blow.

It was all she could do not to gather them *both* in her arms.

"I'll be right back." Feeling Lucas's eyes on her, she retreated to the kitchen and wilted against the sink, resting her forearms on the old-fashioned porcelain basin for support.

A few minutes later, she sensed Lucas's presence and quickly straightened. "How is Max doing?"

"Fine." Lucas glanced over his shoulder. "Racing the wise men's camels across the rug. When I left, Bob was in the lead."

Erin tried to summon a smile but failed. She waited for Lucas to explain. He waited for her to ask.

Lucas's ragged exhale finally broke the silence that stretched between them.

"I should have…" He paused and tried again. "I'm sorry you had to see that."

"What, exactly," Erin said carefully, "did I see?"

Lucas looked away and for a moment she thought he wasn't going to answer.

"Max went through a recent…trauma." He lowered his voice. "I think some of the things he remembers work their way into his dreams. He wakes up screaming but doesn't seem to be aware of anything around him. It's like he's still stuck in the nightmare."

Erin remembered the terror locked in Max's eyes. "Does it happen a lot?"

"Once or twice a week up until a month ago, but he's been fine since we got to Clayton. I hoped things were getting better. Time heals all wounds, you know." Some dark chord in Lucas's voice told Erin that he didn't believe it. "Max won't talk about the dreams. Or what he…saw."

"What he saw?"

Lucas shook his head. "Trust me, it sounds like the plot of a movie of the week."

Trust *me,* Erin wanted to say. Because whatever had happened to Max had affected Lucas, too. All her good intentions of keeping a polite distance between them crumbled beneath the weight of the pain in his eyes.

She waited, silently praying that he would open up to her the way he had in the past.

"His father, my old college roommate, Scott, was shot during a drug deal," Lucas finally said. "The men responsible were afraid Max would be able to identify them. They took him with them when they left."

Cold horror squeezed the air from Erin's lungs, making it difficult to breathe. "Are you saying Max was with his father when it happened? That he witnessed the shooting?"

"Scott called me that morning and said he needed help. I got there as fast as I could but…" Lucas's voice trailed off, leaving Erin to fill in the blanks.

She could barely process what he was saying. "You were there, too?"

"Not in time to save Scott's life. If I'd stayed in touch with him after college, maybe I would have known how bad things were. How deep his girlfriend had gotten him into drugs." Guilt banked in Lucas's eyes, casting a shadow that darkened them to cobalt. "Scott hung on long enough to tell me about Max. He made me promise that I would find him."

"What about Max's mother?"

"Died of an overdose last winter." Lucas's lips twisted. "I promised Scott that I would take care of Max, but I had no idea he expected it would be a permanent arrangement until he asked for a piece of paper."

"I'm sorry." Erin couldn't imagine what he'd gone through.

Max hadn't been the only one touched by the trauma of Scott's death.

"I'm sorry, too." Lucas's fists clenched at his sides. "I'm not sure what Scott's biggest mistake was. Getting mixed up with a bunch of cocaine dealers or giving me custody of his son."

God, help me find the right words to say.

"He knew you'd take good care of Max."

"Okay, *that* was his mistake," Lucas said bitterly. "You can tell I'm clueless when it comes to kids. I have no idea what to do when Max experiences one of those episodes. He doesn't respond to me when

I talk to him. I can't distract him." He sighed. "It's like there's a wall between us. He can't see me. Or hear me. The only thing I can do is set him on my lap and hold him until he comes out of it."

The raw pain in his eyes propelled Erin across the room. Before she thought it through, she took his hand and squeezed.

"It sounds to me like you know *exactly* what to do."

He glared down at her. "I'm not a real parent—I'm a phony. Max would be better off with someone who knows what they're doing. I'm totally winging it here."

Erin dared to smile. "From what I've heard, winging it is exactly what parents do."

Chapter Six

"I smell french fries."

Lucas glanced down at Max and saw his button nose quiver in delight.

He should have known better than to walk past the Cowboy Café at noon, when the tantalizing aroma of burgers and fries—Max's favorite food—permeated the air.

"Are you hungry? We'll go back to Grandma's house and rustle up some lunch." Lucas wasn't ready to see Erin again so soon. Not when he hadn't totally recovered from the conversation they'd had the night before.

Erin might be under the delusion that he had something to offer Max, but Lucas knew there would come a day when he disappointed the boy, too. The way he'd disappointed his parents. The way he disappointed everyone.

"Yup. French fries." Max repeated the words and

flashed a confident smile, certain that Lucas would come through for him.

Trouble was, Lucas kept remembering that Lisette's freezer contained neat little stacks of plastic boxes filled with nutritional things like chicken soup and spinach lasagna.

"How about a grilled cheese—"

"Lucas!" The door of the Cowboy Café swung open and his cousin Brooke bounded out, a sweet-faced toddler balanced on one hip. "I saw you through the window. Are you and Max coming in for lunch?"

Max's eyes lit up and Lucas figured a grilled cheese sandwich was no longer on the menu.

"We are now."

Brooke's blue eyes sparkled. "Macy Perry is with me and Gabe's son, A.J., but there's plenty of room at our table."

"Great." Just great.

As if Brooke were afraid he would change his mind, she linked an arm through his and tugged him toward the door. "Gabe has a meeting at the mine, so Macy and I decided to take A.J. out for lunch and make a day of it. What are you and Max up to?"

"I met with Bev, the real-estate agent, a few minutes ago."

"How did that go?"

"There isn't much for rent or sale right now." Unless Lucas counted the one place he *didn't* want.

Unfortunately, his last resort was beginning to look like his only option.

"I'll ask around," Brooke offered.

"Thanks." With his free hand, Lucas caught Max lightly by the back of the collar as they stepped inside.

And Lucas fell through a crack in time.

The café looked exactly the same as it did the night he'd left town, from the straight-backed chairs, nicked and scarred from the heels of hundreds of cowboy boots, to the old-fashioned cash register perched on the counter.

"There's Macy. She's holding a table for us." Brooke angled toward the back of the café.

A low, guttural laugh came from the direction of the kitchen, stopping Lucas in his tracks. His head jerked around.

"Jerome Hicks is still—" *Alive?* "Around?"

Brooke wrangled A.J. into a booster chair next to a young girl who flashed a shy smile at him and Max. "Jerome *and* his brother, Gerald."

"Unbelievable."

"They're town icons," she said.

"Don't you mean historical landmarks?"

His cousin choked back a laugh. "I'm going to pretend I didn't hear that."

Lucas remembered the day Erin had hired the two brothers. Her mother had been in the hospital, forcing Erin to make a difficult decision and interview prospective cooks. That evening, she had laughingly told him that it felt more as if *she* were the one being interviewed.

Lucas had been indignant on her behalf. "You'll end up paying more if you hire both of them," he'd told her. "You're doing a great job. You don't need two stubborn, retired ranch cooks telling you how to run things when your mom isn't around."

"I do need them. But more than that, I think they might need the café," Erin had said simply.

"I get it. You're collecting strays again."

Erin had grinned but didn't deny it. The next day, Gerald and Jerome Hicks had taken over the kitchen of the Cowboy Café.

Max scrambled onto a chair and Lucas slid in beside him. A bottle of ketchup and mustard flanked the metal napkin holder like bookends, just the way he remembered. He ran his thumb over a set of initials etched in the corner of the table.

ST and LC.

The letters hit him like a spray of buckshot.

Susie Tansley and Lucas Clayton.

Clayton was too small. No matter how hard he tried to escape the past, there it was. Laughing in his face.

Someone might have linked his and Susie's initials, but they'd never been a couple. It had all been a lie, just like her pregnancy. He had a hunch it had been part of a coordinated effort by Susie and good old cousin Vincent to damage his reputation. The trouble was, that time it had actually worked.

For several weeks, Susie had followed him around, openly flirtatious and telling anyone who would listen that they were a couple.

Erin believed Lucas when he'd said that he wasn't cheating on her. She wanted to squelch the rumors once and for all by letting everyone know they had been secretly dating for the past six months, but Lucas wouldn't let her.

He'd dug in his heels and told Erin that anyone who really knew him would realize he wouldn't get involved with a girl as phony as Susie.

Maybe he wouldn't have been so stubborn if he'd known that his own mother would be one of the people who believed the worst.

He could still see the expression on Lisette's face when he'd walked into the kitchen after school and found her and Susie sitting at the kitchen table together.

Disappointment—not disbelief. As if he'd suddenly become the person his father had predicted he would be...

"Hey!" A menu waved in front of his face. "Earth to Lucas. Come in, Lucas."

"Are you always this sassy?" he growled, even though he was grateful that his cousin's teasing comment momentarily chased the shadows away.

"I'm the youngest. I can get away with it," Brooke said smugly. "Have you met Macy yet? Her mother, Darlene Perry, was the part-time secretary at Clayton Christian Church."

"I don't think so." Lucas aimed a polite smile at the young girl sitting next to Brooke and felt a ripple of shock. It was like looking at a miniature version of his cousin. Long blond hair. Hot-pink glasses framed eyes as blue as a summer sky.

"It's nice to meet you, Macy. I'm Lucas and this little guy is Max."

"Hi." The girl's wide smile coaxed a dimple out of hiding.

His gaze cut to Brooke and she shook her head in a subtle warning. So, he wasn't the first one to notice the resemblance.

Was that the reason he'd been hearing Macy's name come up in conversation over the past week? His mother had mentioned that Darlene Perry was terminally ill. He'd assumed everyone had taken the girl under their collective wing out of Christian duty.

But maybe it was because they suspected she was *family*.

"Hey, Kylie!" His cousin waved to someone behind him. "We need a few more menus."

One of the knots loosened inside of Lucas's chest.

Maybe Erin wasn't here—

"Can I take your order?"

She was here.

"Erin!" Without warning, Max clambered over Lucas and launched himself into her arms.

Erin recovered faster than the rest of them.

"Hey, cowboy." Her cheeks turned pink, but Lucas

wasn't sure if it was from embarrassment or the fact that Max was clinging to her neck like a stuffed hanging monkey with Velcro hands, reducing the flow of oxygen to her brain. "What can I get you today?"

"French fries," Max said promptly.

"Coming right up." Without missing a beat, Erin shifted Max to her hip and pulled a note pad out of her apron pocket. "What would the rest of you like?"

Friendly but businesslike. And careful not to make eye contact with him.

Who could blame her, after the way he'd rejected her attempt to comfort him the night before.

She'd reached out to him and he had pulled away.

Over the years, Lucas hadn't let himself harbor regret, convinced that leaving Clayton after graduation had been the best decision. Not only for him, but for Erin.

Looking at her now, it occurred to him that maybe the move hadn't been as bold and daring as it seemed at the time. Maybe he'd been exactly what Erin had accused him of the night he'd packed his bags.

A man who wasn't embracing the future, but rather running from the past.

The thought didn't sit well.

"Lucas?" The toe of Brooke's boot connected with his shin. "You haven't even opened the menu yet."

"A double hamburger, pickles, mustard and extra ketchup," he said automatically.

Brooke grinned up at Erin. "I guess he didn't need to look at a menu."

"I'm sure it hasn't changed, either," Lucas muttered. He realized how that sounded when Brooke's eyebrows shot up into her hairline.

And then he saw Erin's stricken expression.

Erin jotted down Lucas's order, careful to keep her smile in place.

She knew he'd spoken the words without thinking.

That was the trouble. In that simple statement, Lucas had revealed what he thought about the café.

It hadn't changed a bit.

He probably thought the same thing about her.

She still wore her hair in a ponytail. Preferred jeans and cotton shirts over dresses and high heels. No doubt Lucas looked at her in the same way he'd looked at the café and found both of them wanting.

She'd never attended college. Never experienced life outside of Clayton. She owned a café that catered to roughneck cowboys and locals who were more interested in food that "stuck to their ribs" rather than teased their palate.

After her mother passed away, Erin had thought about remodeling. Updating the menu. She'd come to the conclusion that her customers wouldn't want that. They didn't scoff at the familiar—they cherished it. Like it or not, the Cowboy Café fit the tiny community like a favorite pair of boots. Not much to look at but comfortable. Reliable.

So instead of replacing the old display case and tables, Erin had bought a ramshackle place outside of town with plenty of room for the horses she planned to rescue.

It wasn't her original dream—Erin refused to let her gaze drift back to Lucas—but it was something to reach for.

"Erin." Dorothy Henry, proprietress of the Lucky Lady Inn, the local boarding house, waved her napkin to get Erin's attention as she made her way toward the kitchen. "The apple pie is delicious, as usual."

"Delicious. Simply delicious," sang the other two women at her table.

Erin paused to greet the trio of lively seniors who had been meeting at the café for lunch since she was a teenager. "I'll be sure to tell Arabella."

"I think we're due for another snowstorm," Edna Irving spoke up. "I've had a pain in my knee the past few days."

"Don't listen to her, honey. Edna always has a pain in her knee," Dorothy said.

Erin laughed with them, knowing it was expected.

"Excuse me, Erin." Someone hailed her from the table behind them. "I'd like a refill on my coffee."

Erin recognized the smoky voice without turning around. Katrina Clayton Watson, Arabella's mother, had drifted into town a few months ago after a ten-year absence. She'd moved in with Arabella, Jasmine and the triplets but Erin wasn't sure how her friend truly felt about the situation. Arabella had hinted that the relationship with her mother had always been strained but hoped her mother's return meant she wanted to start over.

"I'll be right back with a fresh pot, Kat," Erin promised.

She'd had a difficult time warming up to the woman, too. More than once, she'd heard Kat openly critique her daughter's parenting skills. She also made no attempt to hide her disapproval over Jasmine's upcoming wedding, and Erin had the feeling that Kat was jealous of the close relationship between Arabella and the younger woman.

Kat's gaze lit on Erin as she returned with the coffeepot. Something in the woman's pale green eyes always reminded Erin of a cat ready to pounce.

"You don't seem like your cheerful self today, dear." Kat tilted her head to the side, setting the faux rubies in her chandelier earring swinging like a pendulum. "Is something wrong?"

"No. Everything is fine." Erin might have gotten away with the claim if her hands hadn't been shaking. And she hadn't sloshed coffee over the side of the cup.

"Mmm." Kat made a point to blot up the spill with the corner of her napkin. "I thought Lucas had complained about something. You looked a little flustered when you left their table just now."

"Can I get you anything else besides a refill on your coffee?"

Kat wasn't so easily distracted. She glanced over at Lucas's table. "It appears that my nephew hasn't changed a bit, has he? Still as restless and brooding as ever, like a bronco trapped in a holding chute."

The tinkling laugh that followed the statement set Erin's teeth on edge. She would have moved on but it was obvious that Kat wasn't finished chatting yet.

The woman picked up a spoon and idly began to stir her coffee. "Arabella shooed me out of the house today so she and Jasmine can discuss the wedding plans. I told them I'd be willing to help but…" She shrugged. "They don't need me."

Knowing how sweet-tempered Arabella was, Erin doubted that she had "shooed" her mother out of the house.

"Trust me, Kat," she said quietly. "A girl always needs her mother."

To her astonishment, Kat reached out and patted her hand. "I was sorry to hear that Gloria passed away."

"Thank you—"

"Although to be honest, I'm surprised you didn't sell the café and get out of Clayton while you had the chance."

Erin didn't hold that against her. In all fairness, a lot of people had been surprised when she'd stayed on.

Herself included.

"Clayton is my home. I can't imagine living anywhere else."

"How sweet." Kat bared her teeth in a smile. "Some people are so…easy to please."

Two insults in the space of five minutes.

Help, Lord.

Rescue came a second later in the form of a familiar bellow from the kitchen.

"Order up!"

"Please excuse me, Kat."

"Of course, of course." Kat took a delicate sip from her coffee cup and dismissed Erin with a casual wave. "I wouldn't want to keep you from your work."

That's exactly what she'd been doing, but Erin smiled. And then she walked back to the kitchen and hugged Jerome, who began to sputter and spit like grease on a griddle. "Hey now! What's all this?"

"This—" Erin straightened the frayed collar of the cook's chambray shirt. "—is about remembering that God answers our prayers."

Jerome snorted. "Was there any doubt?"

Erin pressed a kiss against the grizzled cheek. "No. Not really. But it's always good to be reminded."

Brooke waited until Erin was out of earshot before leveling both barrels at Lucas. "Okay, what was that about?"

It was about him trying not to let Erin know how much she affected him, that's what it was about. But Lucas couldn't tell Brooke that. She was engaged to Gabe Wesson, caught up in the whole notion of happily-ever-after.

"I didn't mean to insult Erin," Lucas muttered. "I think this town brings out the worst in me."

He was surprised he said the words out loud. Even more surprised when Brooke nodded as if she understood.

She slid a look at Macy, who was entertaining the boys with a herd of tiny plastic horses she'd emptied out of a bright pink purse.

"At first I hated the thought of coming back, too," she said in a low voice, her expression serious. "But now I thank God that Grandpa George drew up that will—"

"And dangled a large sum of money and all that land in front of everyone like a carrot," Lucas interrupted.

To his surprise, Brooke didn't scold him for being cynical.

"Everyone came back to Clayton for different reasons. Just like we all stayed away for different reasons," she said softly. "All I remembered were the bad things that happened. I blamed myself for Lucy's death. Losing my dad in the accident and then Mom a few years later…it cast a shadow over everything."

Lucas shifted his weight in the chair, not sure

what to say. Brooke's little sister, Lucy, drowned in a tragic accident when they were kids, but he'd had no idea she blamed herself. His cousin had been a child herself at the time.

And caught up in his own grief over his father's death, Lucas had sometimes forgotten that the accident had also claimed the life of his uncle, George Jr. The brothers' deaths rocked the foundation of both families. The pain that should have bonded them had sent the cousins scattering as soon as they were old enough to leave.

"That's why I don't look back. It's better that way."

"I used to think so, too," Brooke admitted softly. "But then I realized I was also closing the door on the good things. Reverend West said that Grandpa changed when he found out he was dying. He made things right with God and he wanted to make things right between us."

Too little, too late, Lucas wanted to argue. Some things were so damaged, they were beyond fixing.

Lucas found his gaze drifting back to Erin.

Even if a man wanted to.

"Me and Zach and Viv, we all had our reasons for coming back and maybe they weren't so noble in the beginning," Brooke admitted. "But now it's less about getting something and more about discovering what we already *have.* Over the past six months, I've fallen head over heels in love."

Brooke saw his expression and chuckled. "Not

only with Gabe. With the town…and the people."
She slipped her arm around Macy's shoulders.
"Maybe you will, too, Lucas."

"If I remember correctly, falling in love wasn't
listed in the terms of the will," Lucas said drily.

"Not in the will, no," Brooke agreed. "But you
never know what *God* has planned."

Chapter Seven

"The closed sign is in the window. We are officially off duty and my feet are officially killing me." Kylie was already untying her apron as she breezed into the kitchen. "I think everyone in Clayton stopped by today for a cup of coffee and one of Arabella's cinnamon rolls."

Not everyone, Erin almost said. She hadn't seen Lucas for several days.

Not that she'd been looking for him.

"When she stops in tomorrow, tell her we have orders coming in for her Christmas tea cakes." Erin added a pumpkin pie to the picnic basket on the counter.

"That looks good." Kylie took a peek inside the wicker container. "Are you giving out samples?"

"Not this time." Erin smiled. "Reverend West called early this morning and asked if I'd put together a meal on behalf of the Church Care Committee. I'm going to drop it off at the Halversons on my way home tonight."

Kylie stripped off her apron and hung it on a hook near the sink. "I thought Archie and Lorraine were selling the house and moving down south."

"I thought so, too, but Lorraine didn't bounce back right away from her last treatment of chemo. Maybe they decided to wait until after Christmas." Erin tied a red satin bow around the handles of the basket. The elderly couple were not only regulars at the café, they happened to be her closest neighbors. Erin hoped the added touch would brighten their day, especially if Lorraine wasn't feeling well.

"Let me know if there's anything I can do," Kylie offered.

"Mmm." Erin tilted her head. "Between waitressing, planning Jasmine and Cade's wedding and spending time with a certain deputy sheriff?" she teased.

"Hey, I learned to multitask from the best," her friend shot back.

"Who would that be?"

"I wonder." Kylie rolled her eyes as Erin turned off the overhead light and they made their way to the front of the café.

As they reached the door, a dark figure loomed in front of the glass, blocking the glow of the street-lamp.

Vincent?

Erin's heart skipped a beat until she recognized Zach Clayton's ruggedly handsome features.

"It looks like you get a police escort home."

Kylie laughed. "He's off duty. We're going to Darlene's house to help Macy decorate their Christmas tree this evening."

"That sounds like fun."

"It will be. We promised her that we would make this Christmas extra special for Macy."

There was no need to ask why. Everyone hoped she would be able to spend the holiday with her daughter, but Darlene's health continued to decline rapidly.

"Good evening, ladies." Zach's smile encompassed both of them but the light in his eyes was for Kylie alone.

After Erin locked the door, he stepped forward and gave the knob a twist to make sure it was secure for the night.

"I thought you were off duty," she teased him.

"Sorry." Zach shrugged. "Habit."

"That's what he says when I accuse him of keeping me under surveillance." Kylie heaved a long-suffering sigh but Erin could tell she didn't mind the attention.

And Zach didn't appear the least bit guilty. "You better get used to it," he murmured. "I plan to keep an eye on you for the rest of my life."

Kylie stood on her tiptoes and pressed a kiss against his rugged jaw. "Promise?"

The look that passed between the couple was warm enough to melt the snow on the ground.

Erin coughed. "Ah, well…good night, you two."

Kylie tore her gaze away from her fiancé and gave Erin a sheepish smile. "See you tomorrow."

"Give Macy a hug for me."

"Sure thing."

Zach's arm went around Kylie's waist and he tucked her against his side as they walked to his vehicle.

Erin tried not to feel envious. She'd never thought Vincent was good enough for Kylie and had prayed often that God would somehow reveal his true character.

Mr. Jones, Kylie's father, had been swindled by Vincent's grandfather after he'd partnered with him in a business deal. When Kylie dropped out of college and returned to Clayton to help her family, Vincent had hinted that if she'd agree to marry him, her family would no longer struggle financially. Kylie had tried to convince herself that she could learn to love Vincent, but when she'd caught him kissing another woman on their wedding day, she realized she couldn't spend the rest of her life with him.

Kylie had been cautious about Zach Clayton at first, but after watching them interact, Erin knew without a doubt that her friend and the handsome deputy were meant to be together.

She, however, had packed dreams of romance away a long time ago. The cowboys who frequented the café flirted with her, and once in a while one of them would gather the courage to ask her out. Erin always declined, using the excuse that she didn't have time to go out, her schedule was too crowded.

And her heart was too crowded with memories of Lucas Clayton. They took up so much space, Erin doubted there was room for anyone else.

It was dark by the time she pulled up to the log home, but lights glowed in the windows. Retrieving the wicker hamper from the backseat, she lugged it up the shoveled walkway to the front door.

The front door that was usually bedecked with an evergreen wreath this time of year.

A frown pleated Erin's forehead. She hoped that didn't mean that Mrs. Halverson's health had taken a turn for the worse. Her husband had retired the year before and the couple was anxious to relocate to Florida to be closer to their daughter.

Because, unlike Lucas Clayton, there were people who *wanted* to be near family.

Erin made a fist inside of her mitten and rapped on the door.

"Merry—" The rest of the greeting died in her throat when the door swung open.

Lucas stood on the other side.

"It's you." His expression changed from irritation to relief. Before Erin could blink, Lucas had yanked her inside the cabin. "I need your help."

"I'm supposed to deliver a meal to the Halversons."

Now it was Lucas's turn to frown. "That's going to be a long drive. They left for Florida yesterday."

Had she misunderstood Reverend West's message? When he'd asked her to deliver the meal to her neighbors, Erin had assumed he'd been talking about the Halversons, but it was possible he had meant the Morgan family, who lived a few miles farther to the north.

"Something smells good." Lucas reached for the basket.

Erin took a step back and tightened her grip on the basket.

"This isn't for you. I'm on the Church Care Committee and we deliver meals to people who are sick. Or new—" To the community.

Oh. No.

It was a distinct possibility that Reverend West might consider Lucas Clayton a newcomer.

"I'm sick of peanut butter and jelly sandwiches—that has to count," Lucas said. "You can leave but there's no way I'm letting you take that basket with you."

Erin was dimly aware of Lucas wrestling the picnic basket from fingers that had suddenly gone numb.

"I didn't know you'd moved in." *Next door. To me*.

"Everything happened pretty fast." Lucas strode across the room with his prize, set it on the counter and lifted the lid.

"The condo the Halversons bought in Florida was completely furnished, so they took their personal possessions and left the rest. The real-estate agent told me they wanted to settle into their new place before Christmas."

Erin began to inch toward the door and her foot landed on something hard. A siren went off. She looked down and saw a plastic police car at her feet, tiny red-and-blue lights blinking.

For the first time, she noticed the mountain of toys heaped in the center of the rug. It wasn't the end-of-the-day roundup, either. Most of the toys looked to be in their original packaging.

Lucas followed her gaze. "Arabella insisted that Max spend the evening with her and the triplets so I would have time to wrap these gifts. The way it's been going, I'm tempted to call and tell her not to bother bringing him back until tomorrow."

"Max isn't here?" Erin tried not to let her disappointment show. She didn't know why the little boy had taken what Gerald Hicks would have called "a shine" to her, but the feeling was mutual. Max was adorable.

"This stew is still hot." Lucas looked ready to swoon. Maybe he hadn't been exaggerating when he said he'd been living on peanut butter and jelly sandwiches.

Erin refused to let herself feel sorry for him. Or smile. "You have to share it with Max."

Lucas looked up and somehow his blue eyes

looked even bluer. "Max is eating supper with Arabella and Jonathan. And the—" he winced as if he had a difficult time even saying the word. "—triplets."

"Then I guess it's all yours."

Lucas met her eyes. "Or I could share it with you."

Had he just invited her to stay for dinner?

Erin fumbled with a button on her coat. "I don't think—"

"And you could help me wrap these presents before Max gets home."

So that was it. Lucas wanted her help, not her company.

"I really should get home." She wanted to stay. "Winston is waiting for his daily walk."

"Winston doesn't walk," Lucas said bluntly. "I can tell."

Erin lifted her chin. "Are you hinting that my dog is overweight?"

"No. As a veterinarian, I'm giving you my professional opinion. Your dog *is* overweight." Lucas peered into the basket again. "If you stay, I'll throw in a piece of pumpkin pie."

Erin couldn't help it. She laughed. "You're terrible."

"And you're a member of the Church Care Committee, right?" He arched a golden eyebrow.

"Yes."

"So start caring," he retorted.

"Fine. I'll help you wrap Max's presents."

"And I'll make dinner." The Clayton dimple made an appearance.

It was hard—no, impossible—to keep her emotions in check when Lucas was standing three feet away from her with that roguish smile on his face. And a piece of tape stuck in his hair.

With his guard down, he looked more like the Lucas she remembered from high school. The young man who'd shared his thoughts and dreams, vented his grief and frustration.

The Lucas Clayton who had shared his heart and stolen hers in the process.

The worst part?

Erin wasn't sure she wanted it back.

After the thoughtless comment he'd made in the café, Lucas hadn't expected Erin to speak to him again, let alone show up at his door. But now that she was here, he wasn't about to let her get away.

When Arabella arrived to pick up Max, she'd left a large sack of toys along with whispered instructions to wrap them before they got back. She'd even put tape and several tubes of wrapping paper adorned with skating penguins in the bag with the toys.

He'd used up half the tape in his first attempt and somehow ended up with a misshapen package that looked as if it had been run over by a herd of wild mustangs.

Erin shook her head and the movement set her

ponytail into motion. "It looks like you bought out the entire store."

"What you are looking at is a coordinated effort by my meddling cousins and their significant others to make sure that Max has a decent Christmas."

"That's sweet."

Sweet? To Lucas, it only proved his family wasn't convinced he had this whole "dad thing" down yet. He might be upset—if it wasn't the truth.

Every day—no, every hour—he was hit with the magnitude of his decision to adopt Max. He had no idea how Arabella coped with being a single parent, to *triplets* no less, and yet she somehow managed to juggle a home-based business and family while adding him and Max to the mix.

Lucas had put in a full day administering vaccinations at one of the nearby ranches and then went to pick up Max from Brooke's house. On his way home, Arabella had called his cell phone and informed him that she wanted Max for the evening.

He didn't know whether to be relieved or offended by his family's intervention.

"What time do you expect Max back?" Erin was asking.

Lucas glanced at his watch. "Fifteen minutes ago."

Her golden-brown eyes widened. "Then I better start wrapping." She plopped down on the rug and began to separate the toys into piles.

Lucas decided the safest place to be at the moment was somewhere Erin wasn't. Did she realize what an enchanting picture she made sitting cross-legged in front of the fire, her forehead puckered in concentration?

He took his time searching the cupboard for dishes until a ripple of laughter washed over him, melting his defenses like a warm Chinook wind coming down from the mountains.

"What's so funny?"

"I think you're right about everyone chipping in." Erin held up the police car. "This one has to be from Zach...and Jack must have picked out the action hero on the four-wheeler."

Maybe setting the table could wait. Lucas wandered over and lowered himself onto the rug beside her. He picked up a tiny plastic grocery basket filled with fake food. "Vivienne?"

Out of all the cousins, Vivienne's return had been the most surprising. Years ago she had shed her small-town roots along with her cowboy boots and studied to be a gourmet chef, eventually settling in New York City. As far from Clayton as Venus is from Mars.

Erin's eyes sparkled. "Bingo."

Something pink snagged his attention. Lucas leaned closer to investigate and unearthed a tea set. He hadn't known there were so many different shades of pink in the world. "Zach always did have a twisted sense of humor."

"I don't think it was Zach." Erin grinned. "My

guess is that Arabella's triplets want to have something to play with other than trucks when they visit."

Erin said the words as if his family dropping by for a visit would be a natural occurrence now that he was back in Clayton.

Lucas had expected his cousins would feel the same way he did about Grandpa George sentencing them to a year in Clayton. They would serve their time, then pack up and move on.

From what he'd witnessed, the opposite was true. His cousins weren't simply surviving—they appeared to be thriving.

If Lucas didn't know better, he'd think there was something in the water.

"Aww, look at this." Erin scooped up a teddy bear and pressed it against her cheek. "Macy must have picked it out. She loves stuffed animals."

Knowing how Lucas had reacted over the tea set, Erin waited for a biting comment while she studied the adorable toy. The bear's fur was soft as down and a patchwork heart had been stitched on its chest.

She glanced up and was amazed to see a wave of color creeping up his neck and surging over the blade of his jaw.

"It's from me." Lucas reached over and plucked it out of her hand. "I thought that maybe having something to sleep with would…"

"Stop the nightmares," she finished.

"It's worth a try."

The casual shrug that accompanied the words didn't fool Erin for a minute.

His family had bought gifts they thought would entertain a four-year-old boy. Lucas had picked out something he thought that Max *needed*. Whether or not Lucas was ready to admit it, he wasn't simply Max's guardian, a role he had taken on with the stroke of a pen. Max had grabbed hold of his heart.

"It's a great idea," Erin said softly.

"You think so?" The flash of vulnerability in Lucas's eyes was further proof he wasn't as impervious to human emotions as he pretended to be. "All this stuff is so…new."

"New can be good." Erin immediately regretted the words. "Never mind. I know what you're thinking," she added in a rush. "That statement is funny coming from someone who never left Clayton and who works in the same place she did in high school and still wears her hair in a ponytail…"

She ran out of breath. Because Lucas had suddenly shifted his weight, shrinking the distance between them.

His expression underwent a subtle change as he reached out and gave Erin's glossy ponytail a gentle tug.

"That's not what I was thinking."

Chapter Eight

Erin's heart stopped as Lucas's fingers continued their exploration, grazing a path down the curve of her jaw...

"Lucas, I'm back...guess what!" The door burst open and Max charged in, Jonathan Turner a step behind him.

Erin vaulted to her feet, sure that her face matched the color of her hair.

Max spotted her and changed direction. "Erin's here!" He dashed around the presents she and Lucas had just finished wrapping and hugged her.

"Sorry we're late," Jonathan said. Unlike Max, he didn't appear the least bit surprised to discover Erin in Lucas's living room. "We had an errand to run."

As far as Erin was concerned, Jonathan's timing had been perfect.

Erin didn't know the doctor very well, but over the past few months he had made an impression on the citizens of Clayton. And Arabella.

Jonathan had shown up in town a few months earlier, searching for the eighteen-year-old niece he hadn't known existed. That girl turned out to be Jasmine Turner, an at-risk teenager Arabella had taken into her home and who soon would be marrying Cade Clayton. Jonathan had wanted to meet his late brother's child and convince her to return to Denver, where he practiced, but had ended up staying in Clayton instead.

Erin knew the man had been vocal in his opinion that Jasmine not get married so young, but she'd eventually won him over. And Arabella had won his heart.

"Presents," Max breathed, finally noticing the mound of gifts they hadn't had time to hide. "Jessie an' Jamie an' Julie gots presents under their tree."

"Right. A tree," Lucas murmured.

"Ours is bigger." Max hopped up and down, his boots depositing clumps of snow onto the rug.

"Ours?" Lucas's eyebrows dipped together.

Max nodded vigorously. "A'bella said we have a house now so we needa tree."

"Is that what Arabella said?" Lucas looked at Jonathan for confirmation.

The doctor shrugged. "Hey, I'm just the chauffeur. And the tree delivery guy."

"You brought it *with* you?" Lucas stared at Jonathan.

"That's right." Jonathan stared right back.

Max appeared unaware of the subtle undercurrents in the room. He stood patiently while Erin knelt down and unzipped his coat. "We gotta decorate it. Like Erin's tree."

Erin didn't have time to feel flattered.

"No tree," Lucas said under his breath, "is going to look like Erin's tree."

Not fair! Erin thought.

Since Jonathan wasn't looking her way, she crossed her eyes and made a face at Lucas.

Leave it to Erin to lighten the moment.

She had always been good at diffusing volatile situations. Lucas remembered there'd been a lot of those in the eight months they'd dated.

But you aren't dating anymore, Lucas reminded himself sternly.

So why had he touched her? No, why had he almost *kissed* her?

He focused his attention on Max, who'd detached himself from Erin's side and flopped on the floor, staring at the presents as if he'd never seen such a bounty.

It struck Lucas that given Max's home environment most likely he hadn't.

Discouragement rolled through him. There were so many things Max needed. How did a guy even begin to fill those holes?

And now he had to disappoint Max again.

"We can bring the tree in but I'm afraid we won't

be able to decorate it, buddy," Lucas said. "I don't have any ornaments or lights."

Jonathan cleared his throat. "As a matter of fact, you do."

"A'bella had extra," Max chimed in.

Good old cousin Arabella, Lucas thought, as he left Max in Erin's capable hands and followed Jonathan out the door.

Lucas stopped dead in his tracks, tracing the dark shape of a mammoth tree strapped to the top of Arabella's vehicle. "You've got to be kidding."

"Talk to Max." Jonathan flashed what could only be described as a wicked smile. "He picked it out."

"Maybe I should talk to Arabella," Lucas muttered.

Jonathan's smile faded. "Your family cares about you, Lucas. They want to help. My advice? Let them."

That was easier said than done. After severing ties with Clayton, Lucas had gotten adept at avoiding commitment. He might be alone at the end of the day, but there was no one to disappoint, either.

Jonathan retrieved a box of ornaments from the backseat while Lucas untied the tree. The two men dragged it up to the cabin. Once they got it inside, Jonathan said goodbye and fled.

The traitor.

Lucas had faced angry cattle, crabby horses and even the occasional bull-headed rancher, but a fragrant evergreen in the middle of the living room had him at a loss.

Max came to his rescue. "You should put it over there." He pointed to the corner near the window.

Erin nodded. "That's a great idea, Max. Then I can see the lights when I drive home at night."

Erin and Lucas wrestled it into place while Max pulled a string of lights from the box of decorations.

"These go on first." He shook them at Lucas, who bore the full weight of the tree against his shoulder.

Lucas grunted. "Not yet, buddy."

"Ah…do you have a tree stand?" Erin's eyes twinkled at him between a gap in the fragrant branches. "Not that you're not doing a great job, but you might get tired of holding it in place for the next two weeks."

Max giggled.

"Knowing Arabella, I'm sure we do," Lucas said drily.

"I'll be right back." Erin returned a moment later holding the tree stand up like a trophy. "You were right."

Lucas knelt down to secure the tree in the stand. Surrounded by the sweet scent of the needles, he tried to remember the last time he'd put up a Christmas tree.

He didn't have to go back further than his freshman year of high school.

"Lucas, you have to help me put up the tree," his mother had said, taking on the wounded expres-

sion that never failed to open a floodgate of guilt. *"You're the man of the house now."*

Seven little words that struck a match against the anger simmering below the surface of his emotions.

"I'm tired of you saying that," he'd shouted. *"I'm not the man of the house. I'm* not *Dad. I'm not going to be a doctor. I'm not going to church and pretend that I buy all the stuff the pastor preaches about peace and goodwill to men, either."*

He'd stormed out of the house and slept in his truck that night.

Merry Christmas.

Lucas hadn't celebrated Christmas for years, but he had to change that. For Max's sake, he had to do this right.

Lucas slid out from under the tree just in time to see Erin reaching for her coat.

Max rushed to her side. "Where ya goin', Erin?"

"I have to go home now, sweetheart. It's getting late."

Max tugged on her sleeve, his expression earnest. "But you gotta help us put on the lights. And the oranments."

Erin smiled but didn't correct him. "I think that's something you and Lucas should do together."

"But we *want* you to stay, don't we, Lucas?" Max looked to him for confirmation.

Maybe it was a mistake to spend time with Erin. Maybe her smile fanned a flame that had never quite burned all the way out. Maybe he was being a nostalgic idiot…

But he wanted her to stay.

"I promised you dinner, remember?"

Erin caught her lower lip between her teeth, an outward sign of the inward battle he'd fought and lost a split-second ago.

"We'll let you put the star on top." Max was smart enough to know when someone was teetering on the edge of a decision. "Jessie says that's the most important job."

Lucas was impressed with the way Max operated. Especially when Erin hugged the boy and brushed a kiss against his downy head. "In that case," she whispered, "I'd love to stay."

An internal alarm began to ring, pushing Lucas into gear. He tore his gaze away from Erin. "How about I string the lights while you two find out what else Arabella thought we needed?"

"Okay. Come on, Erin." Max dropped to his knees beside the box and began to sift through the contents.

Lucas could hear their soft giggles as he threaded the lights through the branches.

They formed an assembly line of sorts. Max took the ornaments from the boxes and brought them to Erin, who handed them to Lucas to hang on the tree.

Max kept up a cheerful, rambling monologue of the evening spent with the Arabella and the triplets, detailing everything from the chicken and mashed potatoes they'd eaten for dinner to driving to Jones Feed and Supply to pick out a tree.

"This is a gigantic one!"

"That one doesn't go on the tree," Lucas heard Erin whisper.

Why had she whispered?

Lucas glanced down. Standing on a kitchen chair provided him an aerial view of the comical goings-on below. And right now he wished he had a camera to capture the expression on Erin's face while Max dangled an enormous ball covered in plastic mistletoe two inches from her nose.

"How come?" Max wanted to know. "It was in the box of dec'rations."

"You hang this one in a doorway."

"Why?" he asked in confusion.

"Because it's mistletoe."

Max's face brightened and Lucas knew what he was thinking. He'd been a boy once upon a time.

"Not a missile," he said swiftly. "Mistle*toe.*"

Max's disappointment was palpable as he studied the prickly ball of artificial greens. "Then what's it for?"

Lucas raised a brow at Erin, whose blush continued to deepen with every innocent question.

"Just to look...pretty. See the cute red bow tied on the top? It's meant to enjoy."

Max looked as if he'd enjoy pitching it across the room more than hanging it above a doorway, but he handed it to Erin.

Out of the corner of his eye, Lucas saw her discreetly tuck it back into the box.

If only he could put aside memories of kissing Erin that easily.

"I think we're done." Erin arranged the last present under the tree and stepped back to admire it.

"And I think someone is…" Lucas stifled a yawn. "Tired."

Erin grinned. "I think so, too."

"I meant him." Lucas nodded at the sofa, where Max had curled up with his blanket while they straightened up the living room. "Time for bed, buddy."

Max didn't even protest when Lucas picked him up and draped him over his broad shoulder.

"Erin, too," Max murmured.

Erin didn't know how much more she could take. The last two hours had been…a gift.

Her sides hurt from laughing at Max's antics and her heart was…well, it was *full*. That's the only way she could describe it.

The tree shimmered in the corner, the lower branches—the only ones Max could reach—drooping from the weight of the ornaments. The trunk was a little crooked. Some of the lights blinked and some of them didn't.

Erin thought it was perfect.

She followed Lucas up the stairs to the loft. While he took Max into the bathroom to brush his teeth and change into his pajamas, Erin turned back the covers.

The bedroom was small but cozy, with knotty pine paneling and a wool trapper's blanket decorating one wall. The twin bed had been handcrafted from peeled logs and Lucas's battered Stetson hung on the bedpost.

Max's favorite blanket, folded neatly, crowned the pillow.

A half smile touched Erin's lips.

Lucas might think he wasn't equipped to take care of a small child, but his actions said something else.

He had been awkwardly sweet with Max while they decorated the tree. Patiently answering his questions. Whistling along with the Christmas carols on the radio. And after the last ornament was in place, Lucas had held Max up so he could help her put the star on top of the tree.

It hadn't escaped Erin's notice that Max absorbed any amount of attention like a desert flower soaked up the rain. The boy needed a stable home. Parents who loved him—and each other.

Erin closed her eyes, reliving the gentle glide of Lucas's hand through her hair.

"I thought only horses slept standing up."

Erin's eyes snapped open as Lucas sauntered back into the room, a drowsy Max cradled in his arms.

"I must be tired, too." Erin decided that part was safe to admit.

Downstairs, Lucas's cell phone began to ring.

"That's work." He shook his head. "I'm on call tonight."

"Go ahead and answer it," Erin said, knowing an after-hours call could mean anything from a simple question to an outright emergency. "I'll finish tucking Max into bed."

"Thanks." Lucas shot a grateful look over his shoulder as he jogged out the door.

Erin pulled the covers up to Max's shoulders and watched his eyelids drift shut, his lips pursed in a smile.

She didn't have to close her eyes to imagine her and Lucas as a team. The three of them—a family.

Erin padded down the stairs and heard Lucas talking on the phone. She hesitated, not wanting to intrude on his conversation but it was difficult in the great room, with no walls between them for privacy.

"Everything is great so far, Bev," Lucas was saying. "No, that shouldn't be a problem but try to give me a little advance notice if you book a house showing. My work schedule is kind of crazy…okay, thanks for calling."

Erin's vision blurred even as everything became clear.

"Max is already asleep." She fought to keep her voice steady as she collected her purse and coat.

Lucas frowned. "You're leaving?"

"I have to take care of the animals."

He beat her to the door and held it open. "Thanks for helping out tonight. It meant a lot to Max."

Did it mean anything to you?

Erin didn't ask the question, though, because she already knew the answer.

Lucas hadn't bought the cabin from the Halversons, he'd *rented* it.

Because he had no intention of staying in Clayton.

Chapter Nine

Returning to Clayton had been difficult. Avoiding it was proving downright impossible.

Lucas would have thought that getting a place on the outskirts of town and working as a large animal vet would have taken him outside the city limits more often than in, but his family apparently had other ideas.

As Lucas parked the truck, he saw Mei's face framed in the window of one of the cottages located on the property of their childhood home. By the time he released Max from the booster seat, his sister was waiting for them at the door. At her side, stood an enormous dog with shaggy white fur.

"Don't worry about Moose," she called out. "He's as gentle as a lamb."

Lucas shook his head as Max grabbed his hand. "And as big as a Shetland pony."

Mei grinned. "That, too."

"I'm surprised Mom agreed to let you keep him. She's pretty fussy about these cottages."

"Moose won her over—and Mom's dog, Albert, too," Mei said. "He's just that kind of guy."

"I see that."

Max, who'd been clinging to him as they approached the door, giggled in delight as Moose's pink tongue swiped his chin.

Lucas wrapped an arm around his sister's shoulders and pulled her against him in a quick hug. She clung to him for a moment.

"Thanks for stopping by, Lucas."

He lifted a brow. "You sent me three texts and left two voice-mail messages. I didn't think I had a choice."

His sister smiled sweetly. "You always have a choice. Fortunately, you made the right one."

Given the fact that Mei wouldn't tell him *why* she wanted him to stop by after work, Lucas decided he would be the judge of that.

"You gotta tree!" Max shouted as they followed her inside. "So do me an' Lucas."

"I heard about that." The knowing look Mei slanted in his direction told Lucas that he'd been the topic of conversation at someone's dinner table. Probably Arabella's. He should have been used to it by now. "Would anyone like a cup of hot chocolate?"

"I do!" Max peeled off his coat and dashed across the room to admire the tree, Moose at his heels.

"I'll get us each a cup." Mei nodded toward a chair at the kitchen table. "You. Sit."

Lucas got the feeling this wasn't going to be a quick visit.

"What's up, sis?" he asked bluntly.

"You don't have to look so suspicious. I just need a favor. A *small* one."

"Sure." Lucas pushed the word out, a little afraid of what a favor from one of his family members might involve. Not that he was in a position to protest. Several times over the past week, his sister had taken care of Max. Hopefully, it was something simple. Like hanging a picture on the wall. Or a minor car repair...

"I'm supposed to take Macy out to Erin's tomorrow afternoon to see the foal, but Jasmine and Cade have a premarital counseling session with Reverend West," Mei explained. "They asked Jack and I to go with them. I thought maybe you could take Macy and Max in my place. Max talks about Erin a lot, so I thought he might enjoy spending some time out at her place, too."

Lucas ignored the question in Mei's voice. No way was he going there.

"Tomorrow afternoon?" he repeated, only to gain more time. Before he said no.

"The whole family is invited to Arabella's for dinner after church, so it would be after that."

Lucas had a sneaking suspicion that he and Max were included in that invitation. But church? He hadn't stepped foot in the door of Clayton Christian Church since his father's funeral.

Mei topped each cup with a handful of miniature marshmallows. "Do you already have plans?"

Plans to avoid Erin, yes.

"Actually..." He hesitated, not sure how he could explain why spending time with Erin wasn't a good idea without bringing up the past—and the fact they had one.

When they'd decorated the tree with Max, Erin had seemed at ease. Patient with Max. Teasing Lucas about the way he handled the ornaments as if they were grenades that were about to explode in his hands. Lucas had forgotten how much he had always enjoyed her company.

As they got Max ready for bed, her presence seemed so right in his home. In his life. Almost as if the years they'd been apart had never existed. Her abrupt departure had taken him by surprise.

Lucas had come to the conclusion it was better this way. The more time spent in Erin's company, the greater the possibility that Max would become too attached to her.

And so would he.

But he set his misgivings aside in the face of Mei's obvious disappointment.

"I suppose I could."

A smile lit his sister's onyx eyes. "Thanks, Lucas. I really appreciate it. Christmas Eve is right around the corner and everyone is so busy, but I didn't want to let Jasmine and Cade down. Or Macy, for that matter," she added.

Lucas thought about the little girl with the bright smile. "How is Macy's mother doing?"

"Not good at all but we're doing everything we can to help Macy get through it."

"We" meaning the community? Or the Clayton family?

"She had lunch with Brooke at the café the other day," Lucas said slowly.

Mei nodded. "Brooke promised Darlene that she and Gabe would adopt Macy."

"Brooke? She's only twenty-three years old."

"She and Macy have gotten really close over the past few months," Mei said in their younger cousin's defense. "And Brooke might be young, but she's great with kids. So is Gabe Wesson, her fiancé. You should see him with A.J. He's a great dad."

"I'm sure that's true, but wouldn't it be better if Macy is adopted by family?"

Mei's expression clouded.

"What?"

"She…might be. Adopted by family, I mean" came the quiet response.

The air emptied out of Lucas's lungs. "I guess I shouldn't be surprised that someone in Samuel's family could turn their back on their own child," he muttered.

His sister remained silent.

"Mei?" Lucas regretted the sharpness of his tone when Max looked up.

Mei flashed him a warning look and took one of the cups of hot chocolate over to Max, who'd discovered the carousel music box on the coffee table. "It's hot, sweetie, so take little sips," she said.

Lucas drummed his finger against the table, waiting for Mei as she walked over to the stove and poured two more cups. He had the distinct impression she was stalling.

When she sat back at the table, he found out why.

"This time it might not be one of Samuel's clan."

Lucas could only stare at her. "What are you talking about?"

"Mom…she thinks that Dad might have had an affair with Darlene Perry, Macy's mother, ten years ago."

Dad? Their dad?

"That's crazy," Lucas snapped.

"I thought so, too. At first." Mei took a deep breath. "But she found a note in his pocket after Dad and Uncle George were killed. It had Darlene's name and address written on it. And the word baby."

"That doesn't mean anything." Lucas couldn't believe she was actually willing to explore the idea. "Dad was involved in all kinds of charity work at the church."

"I know." Mei caught her lower lip between her teeth. "But a few weeks ago, Mom confided in me… told me that it wouldn't have been the first time Dad was unfaithful. He'd had affairs before. I remember them arguing at night after we'd gone to bed and Mom always seemed so distant."

Lucas remembered, too, but he'd assumed that he was the cause of the tension in the household.

He flattened his palms against the edge of the table, trying to absorb the impact of what he'd just heard.

Their father, always quick to point out the flaws in others, may have had an affair. And a child out of wedlock.

Vern Clayton's reputation had meant everything to him. How many times had Lucas heard the question "What will people think?" cross his father's lips?

So many that Lucas had eventually stopped caring.

But as difficult as it was to believe his father had broken his vows more than once and gotten involved with Darlene Perry, Lucas couldn't imagine his uncle, George Jr., straying from his marriage vows, either. He and Aunt Marion had always seemed happy together.

But Brooke must have her suspicions if she'd agreed to take Macy in.

"Did anyone ask Darlene? I mean, this would be—" he hesitated, not wanting to sound insensitive to the woman's failing health "—the time to be honest if Macy is a...Clayton."

"I don't know what to think, but I feel bad that

Mom carried this burden alone for so many years," Mei said softly. "It helped me understand why she's been so distant. Mom must have been blaming herself."

"And here all this time I thought she blamed me."

Mei saw right through his wry attempt at humor. "Mom's changed, Lucas. She wants things to be different."

"You can't change the past."

"No, but you can learn from it." Mei reached across the table and took his hand. "I'm sorry, Lucas. I didn't mean to drop the news on you like this, but you've been so busy since you came back. We haven't had much time to talk."

As usual, his sister was cutting him way too much slack.

Since his return, Lucas had deliberately tried to keep his family at arm's length, telling himself that he didn't want to get caught up in all the drama surrounding George Sr.'s will. He'd let phone calls go to voice mail and used his new job as an excuse to turn down dinner invitations.

"Yeah, well, I'm not used to talking," Lucas said. "At least not to people, anyway. The animals I work with don't demand much."

Mei smiled. "You better brush up on your skills before tomorrow then, brother."

"Why?"

"The dinner at Arabella's?"

Lucas's eyes narrowed. "What about it?"

"It's a welcome home party," Mei whispered, as if she were afraid someone would overhear them. "For *you*."

"Be patient, Winston. I'm almost finished," Erin scolded as her dog turned three circles and flopped down in the straw with a long-suffering sigh. She deposited a scoop of grain into Diamond's feeder before closing the stall door.

She'd put in a full day at the café, waiting on the steady stream of Christmas shoppers who stopped in for a cup of coffee or a piece of pie. However, when she returned home, the thought of heating up a bowl of leftover chili and curling up on the sofa— alone—held no appeal.

Erin had changed into her work clothes and spent the last several hours in the barn, mucking out the stalls and sweeping the floor. Changing the bedding where the kittens slept.

If she wasn't mistaken, there was a light bulb that needed to be replaced…

Winston rolled to his feet and barked at her, almost as if he'd read her thoughts.

Erin chuckled. "Okay, okay. I get it. You want to go inside." The trouble was, Erin wasn't ready to go back to the house yet.

Before he'd returned to town, thoughts of Lucas

had only dominated her memories. Now they invaded both her heart and her home.

Especially since he showed up *everywhere* these days.

Whenever Erin was in the kitchen, she remembered the vulnerable expression on Lucas's face when he told her what had happened to Max. When she walked into the living room, she didn't see the Christmas decorations, she saw Lucas on the sofa, his arms wrapped protectively around Max as if he could somehow shield the boy from his fears.

And now, when she looked at her Christmas tree, images of the wonderful evening she'd spent decorating with Lucas and Max returned to torment her.

Why had she been so surprised to discover that he'd rented the cabin next door? Lucas made no effort to conceal how he felt about Clayton. He'd stayed away for years, hadn't he?

Lucas had no intention of returning to his roots. His decision to rent proved he'd only come back to satisfy George's last wishes and claim his inheritance.

And Erin was never going to make it through the next year. Not if that meant seeing Lucas on a regular basis.

And Max.

When he'd planted a kiss on her cheek after she'd tucked him into bed, she'd wanted to hug him and never let go.

Max, she told herself sternly, *not* Lucas.

Lucas she wanted to…shake silly. And *then* hug.

It was obvious that neither time nor a change of scenery had healed the wounds of his past.

What had made her hope that *she* could?

Standing in the doorway of the barn, Lucas saw the weary slump of Erin's slim shoulders and tamped down a surge of anger. At himself.

In the past, he'd always gotten on her case about her overdeveloped sense of responsibility and yet here he was, about to add more weight to the burden she already carried.

Lucas took a step backward, intending to sneak out the same way he had come in. A floorboard creaked, alerting Winston that there was an intruder in the barn. The corgi barked once and trotted toward him, tongue unfurling in anticipation of an impending saliva bath.

Erin's head snapped up and she whirled around to face him.

"Hey." No escaping now. "I saw the lights on."

"Lucas." She didn't move. Didn't even smile.

Lucas found himself wanting the woman that had been at his house the night before. The one who'd blushed at the sight of mistletoe and helped him tuck Max into bed.

He bent down to scratch Winston's ears. "I'm on my way home from Frank Clayton's place."

"I'm sorry," Erin said automatically. She flushed

and caught herself. "Now I'm sorry again. I shouldn't have said that. He is your relative."

"Don't worry about it. He likes to forget that little detail, too." Lucas smiled when Winston flipped over onto his back, exposing his belly for more attention.

"Is Max with you?"

"Not yet. Viv and Cody's sister Bonnie offered to watch him for a few hours while I stopped out at Frank's. One of his geldings went lame and he wanted me to put it down."

Erin's expression went from guarded to dismayed. "But you could save it."

Lucas had to admit he was touched by Erin's confidence in him. It was a lot more flattering than Frank's blatant skepticism that he'd actually earned the title of veterinary doctor.

The man had trailed him to the barn, asking questions about Lucas's new job and dropping veiled references about George Sr.'s will. How it would have been nice if Lucas's grandfather had rewarded the family members who'd stayed in town rather than those who'd left.

It was ironic that Frank didn't realize the ones who had left did so because the ones who'd stayed had made life for George's offspring unbearable.

"Frank didn't want me to." Lucas saw the toe of Erin's boot tap the floor twice and realized she was waiting for an answer. "When I told him it was a degenerative condition, he didn't want to be bothered with the cost and fuss of medication."

"So…you came over to tell me that you had to put Frank's horse down," she said slowly.

"Not exactly. I came to tell you that I bought him." At twice the cost of what a lame horse was going for these days.

"You *bought* him?"

Confession time. "For you."

"For me!" Erin squeaked.

"Don't worry, it'll be joint custody. I'll pay for feed and provide free medical care. If that's okay," Lucas added.

"Frank said he'd drop him off whenever its convenient." For an additional fee, but Erin didn't need to know that.

"But…" Erin's voice trailed off.

"I remembered you said you wanted to rescue more horses like Diamond. I was thinking about it, and while I'm here, I can donate my services for any animals you adopt." Lucas had come to that decision on the drive to Erin's.

He'd already talked to Tweed and got his boss's permission to rip up the bill for delivering Diamond's foal.

Erin's shoulders straightened beneath the bulky coat. "That's very nice of you," she said politely. "I'll call Frank in the morning."

"Great." Lucas knew when he was being dismissed and felt the sting of Erin's less-than-enthu-siastic response to what he'd thought was a generous offer.

What did you expect, a hug?

Her quick exit the night before had proved that Erin didn't want to spend time alone with him for old times' sake. She'd agreed to stay and help wrap gifts because she liked Max, not because of any re-sidual feelings she might still have for Lucas.

Apparently she had room in her life for little boys who wanted to decorate Christmas trees and lame horses that needed a home. But not him.

And Lucas had no one to blame but himself.

Erin spent another hour in the barn, getting the empty stall next to Diamond's ready for the new ar-rival.

"Thank you, Lucas Clayton," she muttered under her breath.

Not that she minded the extra work that another horse would bring. She welcomed it, especially if it took the poor animal away from Lucas's uncle, whose hard-handed methods of "training" his horses were well-known in the area.

No, what she minded was Lucas sauntering back into her life with the full intention of sauntering right back out again.

While I'm here I can donate my services for any animals you adopt.

If Tweed had made the offer, Erin would have been thrilled. But she doubted that Lucas had even realized what he'd said.

The same way he hadn't cared how she would interpret the conversation she'd overheard between him and the real-estate agent.

She sighed and Winston pushed his wet nose against her knee in sympathy.

"Men can be so clueless sometimes," she said. "Present company excluded."

Winston cast a hopeful look at the door.

"We're done for tonight."

Erin flipped off the lights in the barn and stepped out into the moonlit night. Stars winked overhead in the black velvet sky.

If she was lucky, one of them would fall on her head and erase every memory of Lucas Clayton. Then whenever he showed up, she would stare right into those blue eyes…and probably fall in love with him all over again.

The crunch of tires against snow broke the silence.

Winston's tail began to wag. For one heart-stopping moment, Erin wondered if Lucas had returned. Until she saw the red-and-blue light bar on top of the vehicle.

When she saw who hopped out of the driver's side of the squad car, Erin's pulse returned to its normal rhythm and she smiled. "Hey, Zach."

"Erin." Zach returned the greeting but not the smile. "Can you take a ride with me?"

"That depends. Are we going down to the department for questioning?" Erin was teasing but something in Zach's solemn expression ignited a spark of fear. "What's wrong?"

"There's been a fire. At the café."

Chapter Ten

"A fire?" Erin searched the deputy's face, waiting for Zach to admit that he'd been teasing her, too.

"It started in the Dumpster out back," Zach explained. "There's minimal damage to the building itself but I'd like you to come with me and take a walk around the inside so we can see if anything's missing…"

The words dissolved in Erin's ears as she tried to make sense of what he was saying.

Fire. Minimal damage.

Erin swallowed hard against the lump swelling in her throat and making it difficult to breathe.

Emptying the trash was the last responsibility of the day. Had something she'd thrown away accidentally ignited a fire?

"…want to make sure there's no sign of vandalism."

Vandalism?

"What?" Erin's voice thinned. "You think someone set the fire on purpose?"

Zach nodded, his expression grim. "One of the volunteer firefighters found a bunch of rags mixed in with the trash. And it looks as though an accelerant may have been used to start the blaze."

"I'll put Winston in the house and meet you in town." Once she could force her feet to move.

"Maybe you should ride with me," he suggested.

Erin assented with a jerky nod. Zach must have realized that she was too shaken to concentrate on driving. She put Winston in the house and found the deputy sheriff waiting for her just outside the door.

His hand cupped her elbow, steadying her as she got into the squad car. The warm air pumping out of the vents in the dashboard couldn't permeate the chill that had settled in her bones.

Zach was silent for several moments, as if he sensed that she needed time to think. To pray.

"It must have been some kids goofing around. Playing with matches." Erin eventually broke the silence. "They probably didn't mean to start a fire. Right?"

She waited for Zach to agree but he answered her question with one of his own.

"What time did you close up tonight?"

"Seven. The same as always."

"Were you alone?" he asked.

"Kylie got off work at six but Jerome and Gerald left at the same time I did."

"Do you remember who your last customers were?"

Erin tried to visualize the faces of the people who'd sat at the tables she'd cleared. There'd been so many people in and out that day, running errands and doing their last-minute Christmas shopping.

"A few of the guys from the Lucky Lady mine. Mayor Pauley—" Out of the corner of her eye, Erin saw Zach's jaw tighten, an outward sign of how he felt about his distant relative.

The Clayton family had been divided—split down the middle by the animosity that had existed for years between George Sr. and his brother, Samuel. If Lucas and his cousins had refused to return by Christmas and make Clayton their home for a year, the inheritance from their grandfather would have passed to Samuel and his offspring.

That alone would have been enough to cause the rift to widen, but Jasmine and Cade's engagement had added additional fuel to the resentment smoldering between the two sides of the family.

"He was alone for a while, until Charley and Billy Dean Harris joined him. They weren't together long. A few people came in and bought bakery items." Erin tried to match tables and faces. "Your Aunt Kat. She stopped by looking for Arabella."

The woman had also unloaded a litany of complaints about her daughter in the ten minutes she'd lingered at the counter, but Erin saw no reason to mention that.

"You parked in the alley behind the café?"

"Yes." Erin shifted in the seat, uncomfortably aware that this was a police interview, not the polite conversation she and Zach had exchanged in the past.

They reached the city limits and Erin leaned forward, her shoulders tense. Zach had said there was minimal damage, but what exactly did that mean?

"Would you like me to call Kylie and ask her to meet us there?" Zach murmured. "She'd be waiting at the door before I put the car in park."

Erin smiled, knowing it was true. The thought of having her friend close by was tempting but there was no sense in having both of them lose sleep.

"I'll be all right." Erin sent up a silent prayer for strength as Zach pulled up in front of the café.

He held out his hand and Erin dropped the key into his outstretched palm. As soon as Zach disappeared, she sank against the worn upholstery and closed her eyes.

Arson.

Erin could hardly wrap her mind around the word. This was Clayton, Colorado. The people who lived in the area didn't lock their vehicles or their houses. It had to have been some bored kids, messing around the Dumpster with matches.

And an accelerant.

Erin pressed her forehead against the glass, waiting for Zach to reappear. Finally, he appeared in the window and waved at her to come inside.

Shadows danced on the walls as Erin walked through the café. She was comforted by Zach's solid, reassuring presence beside her while she looked around. Nothing appeared to be out of place. No windows had been broken. The safe in her office hadn't been tampered with.

She followed Zach out the back door to the alley where the acrid scent of smoke burned her nostrils. Wet rags littered the snow around the Dumpster. On the exterior wall behind it, black soot had left an ominous stain.

Erin's gaze followed its path to the wooden overhang above the back door and her stomach pitched. If left unchecked, the flames could have spread to the rest of the café.

Zach nodded, as if she'd spoken the thought out loud. "An anonymous call came in," he said carefully. "They told dispatch about the fire and then hung up. Normally when a person calls, they identify themselves and stay on the line until help shows up."

Erin realized that Zach was waiting for her to comment, but she couldn't think straight. She could barely think at all. She imagined the faces of the customers who had come in that day, their pleasant banter rising over the Christmas carols playing on the jukebox.

"I can't believe someone did this deliberately."

"If you can remember anything," Zach urged. "No matter how trivial it might have seemed at the time."

"You're asking me if I remember burning someone's biscuits?"

Zach's lips quirked in a lopsided smile so reminiscent of Lucas's that it suddenly hurt to breathe. He shook his head. "Since I know that doesn't happen on Gerald and Jerome's watch, try to think of something else. Someone who might want to get your attention. Someone who might have a…grudge."

"A grudge? Of course not…" Erin's voice trailed off as Vincent's mocking laughter danced in her ears.

"I want what's mine and Lucas isn't going to cheat me out of it this time."

No.

Erin instantly rejected the thought.

Vincent might have a list of grievances against Lucas, but what would he possibly have against her?

"You thought of someone." Zach had been watching her closely.

"No…it's silly."

"Let me be the judge of that," he said.

She sighed heavily, feeling as if she were back on the playground, tattling on a bully. "Vincent came in around closing time a few nights ago."

Zach's lips flattened. Although the breakup with Kylie had been Vincent's fault, he hadn't made it easy on her after she broke off the engagement. His resentment had continued to grow when it became evident that Zach and Kylie's friendship was developing into something more.

"Did he harass you?"

"Some of the things Vincent said…he made it clear that he's still got it in for Lucas." Erin decided not to mention that Vincent had grabbed her wrist. "But I'm sure it wasn't him. What would he have to gain? I mean, we're not exactly friends, but he has no reason to target me or the café. Lucas and I… there's no connection between us."

"Are you sure?" Zach pressed.

This time, Erin couldn't prevent a thread of bitterness from weaving through the words.

"I'm sure."

"Look, Lucas! There's a Bob in here."

Lucas groaned.

Max understood that to mean he was awake and scrambled onto the bed. "See?"

At that moment, the only thing Lucas could see was the inside of his eyelids. By sheer will he forced them open and squinted several times. Gradually, the blurry object clutched in Max's hand turned into a Christmas ornament. Inside the cavity was a miniature nativity scene and, sure enough, a trio of tiny camels.

"Camels. Right." Lucas yawned and sat up.

Max studied the ornament cupped in his hands.

"Baby Jesus is sleepin' in there." He looked at Lucas for confirmation.

"Yup." Lucas cleared his throat. "That's who it is."

Max looked pleased. "He loves me."

Lucas drew in a careful breath and not because Max's elbow was digging into his ribs. "Did your Grandma Lisette or Aunt Mei tell you that?"

"Uh-uh." Max snuggled closer and the sweet scent of bubblegum shampoo drifted into the air. "Erin."

So, not only had she baked cookies with Max that day, she'd also taken time to share the Christmas story with him. And it was just like Erin to wrap the entire gospel message into three simple words.

He loves me.

As the son of Vern Clayton, missionary doctor, Lucas knew the Christmas story inside out and upside down. He'd memorized verses and played the part of Joseph in the children's Christmas pageant.

For years he'd tried to do everything right. Grades. Sports. Church activities. Every time he would accomplish something, he would look to his father for approval. Approval he never received.

The day Lucas had given up and stopped trying, he'd turned his back on everything his father had stood for. He had tried to pray, but every time he thought of God, it became blocked by an image of his father, arms crossed, glaring down at him.

You disappoint me, Lucas.

"That's Mary and…" Max peered at the tiny figures inside the stable. "Joe."

Lucas choked back a laugh. "Joseph, Max. His name is Joseph."

"Jesus' daddy?"

This was *not* the conversation a man should have with a four-year-old before his first cup of coffee in the morning.

Maybe, Lucas thought darkly, he should call Erin and let her do the explaining. "God is Jesus' father. He's everyone's father, really—"

"'Cause He made us," Max interjected.

"Right." Lucas blew out a relieved sigh, momentarily grateful that Erin had covered that part, too. "God made us. He made everything." Lucas had never stopped believing that, he just doubted he could ever measure up to God's standards. Not when he hadn't even been able to please his earthly father. "But He lives in heaven, so Joseph took care of Jesus and Mary and kept them safe."

"From the bad guys?"

"From the bad guys." Lucas guessed that was a pretty accurate description of King Herod's soldiers.

"An' Joseph 'dopted him?"

Lucas should have been surprised that Max knew the word, but then again, knowing they were the main topic of conversation around his family's dinner table, maybe not.

"Sure, I guess you could say that."

"Like you 'dopted me."

Lucas felt the room tilt.

Over the past few months, he'd been Max's rescuer. His protector. He'd signed his name on some legal documents and become his guardian.

But Max didn't care about promises or legal documents. He didn't need a guardian...he wanted—no needed—a father.

If only Lucas knew how to *be* one.

Winging it is what parents do, Erin had said. If only it were that simple.

"Are you hungry?" Fortunately Max was too young to recognize the tactics of someone desperate to change the subject.

"We're goin' to Aunt A'bella's now? I'm gonna tell Jessie we decorated our tree."

"I meant hungry for breakfast," Lucas said. "We're not going to Arabella's until lunchtime."

Max deflated against him like a punctured balloon. "How come?"

"They won't be home until after church."

Max tilted his head. "What's church?"

Another wave of guilt crashed over Lucas. If he and God had been on speaking terms, Lucas might have thought He was trying to tell him something.

Lucas sighed. "It's where we're going after breakfast."

Chapter Eleven

Erin felt a tug on the hem of her skirt. She glanced down, expecting to see one of Arabella's triplets, but it was Max who stood there, grinning up at her.

"Hi, Erin!"

"Max." Erin bent down and hugged him, while at the same time searching the faces of the people in the sanctuary for Mei or Lisette Clayton, who must have lost track of the little boy when the service ended. "How are you?"

"Hungry."

Erin laughed and ruffled his hair. "The café is closed today, but I'm sure someone will make lunch for you."

"We're going to Aunt A'bella's house to eat. I'm gonna tell Jessie an' Julie an' Jamie—" Max paused to take a breath "—that our tree is bigger than theirs."

Our tree. Erin was touched that he included her

but she wouldn't let her thoughts drift to the evening she'd spent at Lucas's. "I'm sure you'll have fun."

"Are you coming, too?"

The innocent question pulled at the loose threads of her emotions. Zach had invited both her and Kylie a few days ago but after the night she'd had, Erin knew she wouldn't be good company.

"Not today, sweetie." Erin straightened while keeping a protective hand on Max's shoulder. "Where's your Auntie Mei?"

"I don't know."

"Didn't she bring you to—" The next word stuck in Erin's throat and her heart took a slow tumble when a man emerged from the crowd.

Lucas.

He'd replaced his usual jeans and flannel shirt for a pair of tan cargo pants and a moss-green button-down shirt that enhanced the color of his eyes the way the leaves of a cottonwood complimented a summer sky.

Erin had volunteered to work in the infant nursery that morning, so she hadn't seen him come in. As far as she knew, Lucas hadn't stepped through the doors of Clayton Christian Church since his father's funeral.

So what had brought him here today?

"Lucas?" She lifted her hand to flag him down.

The frantic look in Lucas's eyes faded when he saw Max safely tucked against her side.

"Max," Lucas's voice came out in a low growl. "You were supposed to wait for me."

"I was. I'se just waitin' with Erin," Max said reasonably.

Lucas glanced at her. "Thanks for keeping an eye on him. Again. I was talking to Vivienne and Cody Jameson and the next thing I knew Max was… gone."

"They're quick at Max's age." Erin refused to smile at the look of utter bewilderment on Lucas's face that a four-year-old could disappear so quickly.

In fact, it was probably best not to look at Lucas at all, given the fragile state of her emotions. Whether lack of sleep or the stress of knowing how close she'd come to losing the café, tears had been simmering just below the surface all morning.

"Hey, Lucas!" Arabella's voice rose above the hum of conversation in the church foyer. "We're leaving now."

"Okay. Be there in five."

Knowing Lucas would be joining the rest of his family for lunch made Erin even more relieved that she'd turned down the invitation.

"Bye, Erin. Wait for me, Aunt A'bella." Max dashed toward his aunt.

Lucas, however, remained at her side, his eyes shadowed with concern as he stared down at her. "Is everything all right?"

Erin didn't want Lucas to be sensitive. Or kind.

It made it that much harder to keep her distance. "I'm fine."

"You look...tired."

Erin forced a smile. "What every woman wants to hear."

"I'm serious."

And she seriously needed to get away from the man before she launched herself into his arms and released the emotions bottled up inside of her.

Erin had tossed and turned for hours after Zach dropped her off at home. She'd been counting on the fact that a cup of coffee and an extra layer of foundation would hide the damage of a sleepless night.

No one, not even Reverend West, had commented on the shadows underneath her eyes. No one except Lucas—the last person Erin had expected to notice.

Mei swept toward them, stunning in a dress made of mistletoe green velvet. "Are you two setting up a time to get together this afternoon?"

Erin's gaze bounced from Lucas to his sister and back again. "A time to get together?" she repeated.

"Jasmine asked Jack and I to attend a premarital counseling session with her and Cody this afternoon, so Lucas offered to bring Macy out to your place after dinner."

Erin cast a sideways glance at Lucas. "You didn't mention that last night."

"You were together last night?" Mei asked, her eyes alight with interest.

Lucas shifted his weight. "I had to stop by Erin's. It was a...professional call."

"I see." Mei grinned.

No, you don't, Erin wanted to say.

"I was actually planning to come into town later today to buy some more grain at the feed store," she said, grateful for the excuse. "I can swing by Arabella's and pick up Macy on my way home."

A tiny frown marred Mei's smooth forehead. "Are you sure it's no trouble? Lucas doesn't mind."

Even if that were true, which Erin suspected it wasn't, *she* minded. Macy's company would be a nice distraction from her troubles but Lucas would simply be a...distraction. "It's no trouble at all. I'll be there about two o'clock."

Mei linked her arm through her brother's. "I guess you're off the hook."

"I guess so."

The smile Erin aimed at Lucas fell short of its mark when she saw a shadow skirt across his face. If Erin hadn't known better, she would have thought it looked like...regret.

But she *did* know better. Even if Lucas had regrets, it was time to face the truth, once and for all, that Erin Fields wasn't one of them.

There were so many vehicles parked outside Clayton House, Arabella's turn-of-the-century Victorian, that her yard resembled a used-car lot.

If Max hadn't been so excited about seeing the

triplets again, Lucas might have turned the truck around and headed back to the cabin.

A mittened hand battered against the window. "We're here!"

"We sure are," Lucas muttered. He nosed the truck around until it faced the road, in case a quick getaway was in order.

The door opened as soon as his foot hit the top step of the wide, wraparound porch.

"Hi, Lucas. Max. Come on in!" Jasmine Turner stood on the other side of the door. She wore jeans, a hooded sweatshirt and a wedding veil as delicate as a butterfly's wing over her straight brown hair.

Lucas tilted his head. "Did you change the date?"

The young woman grinned at his confusion. "No, it's still Christmas Eve. Macy and the triplets insisted I model my veil for them…and then you knocked. And everyone else is in the kitchen." Jasmine gave a helpless shrug. "Come in and join the chaos."

Chaos was a good word for it, Lucas thought as he peeled off Max's coat and set him loose. He charged down the hall toward the den, where the pint-size members of the Clayton family had gathered in front of the television.

"The triplets couldn't wait for Max to get here." Jasmine took their coats and tried to squeeze them into a narrow closet already bulging with outerwear. "Until recently, a man in this house was a bit of a novelty."

"I'm going to tell Jonathan you said that." A guy in his late teens wandered into the hall. He tucked one arm around Jasmine's slender waist and stuck out his hand. "It's good to see you again, Lucas."

Lucas hesitated a split second before extending his own.

"Same here." Lucas gripped his younger cousin's hand, amazed at the transformation. The last time he'd seen Cade Clayton, the boy had been nothing but arms and legs and missing his two front teeth.

Because of the animosity that divided their families and the difference in their ages, Lucas had never gotten to know Cade, or his step-brother, Jack McCord, very well. But Cade's smile appeared genuine and he lacked the aura of discontentment that seemed to cling to Samuel's side of the family like smoke from a campfire.

His great-uncle had to be as mad as a rabid coyote at the thought of his grandson marrying Arabella's foster daughter.

A high-pitched screech, followed by a loud crash, made all three of them cringe.

"My turn," Cade said and jogged toward the living room.

"We're taking turns?" Lucas muttered.

"It's only fair." Instead of following her fiancé, Jasmine fell into step with Lucas.

"I just wanted to tell you that I think it's great how you took Max in and gave him a home," she said in a low voice. "I don't know what I would have done without Arabella over the past few years. And now I have Jonathan in my life, too. And of course, Cade. God keeps blessing me with family."

Lucas didn't know what to say. He hadn't really thought about family being a blessing before and he certainly hadn't considered that description for himself when it came to Max.

Communication with his parents had been almost nonexistent unless Lucas was getting lectured. His relationship with Mei was complicated. Even though his sister was older, she'd been shy and withdrawn, always in the background of the family portrait. They'd been close as children but time and distance had worked against them. Over the years she'd tried to reach out to him, but Lucas had gotten better at letting go than holding on.

Maybe there had been some good times, but looking for them was like mining for gold. So rare that Lucas wasn't sure it was even worth the effort.

Arabella poked her head out of the kitchen and crooked a finger at him. "There you are, Lucas. Come with me. Real men congregate in the kitchen."

"Because that's where the food is." Jasmine smiled and gave him a playful push in Arabella's direction. "You go and enjoy some adult conversation. Cade and I will keep an eye on Max."

Lucas wasn't sure whether to thank her or not as he walked into the kitchen and immediately found himself surrounded, not only by immediate family, but also their significant others.

Brooke and Gabe Wesson were putting together a relish tray while Vivienne and Cody Jameson sat together at the counter, peeling potatoes. Cody, a local rancher, was Vivienne's new fiancé, according to Mei.

Vivienne's head came up as Lucas entered the room. Her blue eyes sparkled below a fringe of blond bangs and the Clayton dimple came out in full force. "There's our guest of honor now."

"Shh." Brooke shook a carrot stick at her. "He's not supposed to know."

Lucas rolled his eyes. "I know."

"All right. Who told him?" Arabella's eyes narrowed as she made a slow sweep of the room, searching for the guilty party. "Jonathan?"

The doctor's eyes twinkled. "Not me. Doctor-patient confidentiality, you know."

Over Arabella's shoulder, Mei pinched her fingers together and made a zipping motion over her lips. Jack McCord, stationed beside her at the double sink, simply grinned.

"Zach?" Arabella speared him with a look.

"Don't look at me," Zach said. "I've been trained to withhold information."

"You certainly have." Kylie marched into the kitchen with a casserole dish in her hands and sparks in her eyes. "I had to hear about the fire at the café from Dorothy Henry!"

* * *

The sudden uproar from the group drowned out the sound of Lucas's heart hammering against his rib cage.

"What fire?"

"What happened?"

"Was anything damaged?"

"Is Erin all right?"

Zach ducked his head as the questions peppered the air like buckshot and held up his hand in a bid for silence. "The fire started in the Dumpster behind the café last night so there was no damage to the building. Erin was home at the time but I picked her up and took her down to the café. We took a walk through. Nothing appeared to be damaged or stolen."

"Why did you think there would be?" Lucas asked.

All eyes turned in Lucas's direction and the sudden silence proved more unnerving than their questions. Not quite the response he had expected.

"There've been a few—" Jack paused, searching for the right word "—situations lately."

"Situations?" Lucas looked at Zach and dread pooled in his stomach. "What kind of situations?"

"You know what happens if one of us breaks the terms of the will," Zach finally said.

"None of us inherits a thing." Lucas pushed the words out through gritted teeth. "That's why we came back."

"But if life gets…difficult…here and one of us leaves, Samuel's side inherits," Vivienne added.

Lucas knew that, too. "So?"

Brooke sighed. "So life has been getting difficult."

"Define difficult." Lucas kept a tight rein on his impatience.

Vivienne looked at Arabella.

"Jasmine's wedding dress disappeared. We found it later, completely shredded," their older cousin said.

"It sounds like someone doesn't want them to get married." No matter what Lucas's opinion on Cade and Jasmine's upcoming wedding, he couldn't imagine anyone going to such extreme lengths to prevent it.

"There's more," Zach told him.

More? Lucas had already heard enough.

"Zach's gun and badge were stolen a few months ago," Arabella said. "Someone wanted him to look bad."

And Samuel Clayton's side of the family excelled at making others look bad, Lucas knew.

"A bunch of Cody's hired hands got food poisoning. Since I was the cook, I got blamed for it," Vivienne added. "I almost gave up and went back to the city."

The rancher took her hand.

"It wouldn't have mattered," Cody murmured. "I would have brought you back."

Vivienne smiled but it was the last thing Lucas felt like doing.

As the list of offenses against his family increased, so did his anger. He couldn't believe they'd kept all this from him. He shot Mei an accusing look.

"You've had a lot on your plate since you got back." His sister's dark eyes flashed a mute apology, leaving Lucas to wonder if that was the only reason they hadn't kept him in the loop.

"We think someone on Samuel's side of the family has been looking for a...weak link," Brooke explained. "One of us who won't stick it out if things get tough."

Lucas didn't have to ask who they thought that might be. The family prodigal, who'd made no secret of the fact that he would never return to Clayton.

"The fire at the café could have been an accident, though," Arabella pointed out.

"Or it could be my fault." Kylie's shoulders slumped. "I work at the café and Vincent hasn't forgiven me for breaking our engagement."

"That's a definite possibility," Zach agreed. "I can't think of another reason why the person who's been trying to run us out of town would suddenly turned their attention to Erin."

A cold trickle of fear worked its way down Lucas's spine.

He could.

Chapter Twelve

Erin sat in her car, trying to work up the courage to walk up to the door. Even with the windows closed, she could hear peals of childish laughter coming from the house.

Maybe if she honked the horn…it would bring everyone running.

Instead of going home after the worship service, Erin had sought refuge in the café. She'd opened the windows to air out the lingering smell of smoke and tried not to imagine a shadowy figure lurking in the alley.

If Vincent wanted to send out a warning to Lucas, he would have found a better way. She meant nothing to Lucas. Why target her?

The curtains lifted and an elfin face framed in light brown curls appeared in the window and disappeared just as quickly. One of Arabella's triplets was about to sound the alarm.

Erin got out of the car and fought the wind for

control of her scarf. To her relief, it was Kylie who answered the door when she knocked.

And enveloped her in a bone-crushing hug.

"We missed you today," she whispered in Erin's ear. "I heard about the fire. Are you all right?"

"Yes." Erin gasped the word.

Kylie stepped back and eyed her critically, taking in the lavender brushstrokes beneath Erin's eyes.

"You don't look fine," she said with brutal honesty. "We're just finishing dessert but I'm sure there's a piece of Arabella's chocolate cake with your name on it."

Erin backed up. "Thanks, but I think I'll take a rain check. Is Macy ready?"

"I'll round her up. The kids have been playing hide and seek." Kylie grinned. "I guess we'll see if I'm as good as I used to be at that game. Don't you want to wait inside where it's warm?"

"No." Erin said the word so forcefully that Kylie blinked.

"I left the car running."

"Okay." Fortunately, her friend didn't push the issue. "I'll send her out."

Erin was almost to the vehicle when she heard footsteps behind her.

"Erin?" Lucas's husky voice stopped her in her tracks.

She worked up a smile and turned around to face him. "What is it?"

Lucas's gaze swept over her with the critical eye

of a doctor looking for symptoms. She had no doubt he saw them all. The shadows under her eyes. The pallor of her skin. Evidence of a sleepless night.

He took a step forward and for one heart-stopping moment, Erin thought he was going to take her into his arms. He thrust his hands into his pockets instead.

"Why didn't you tell me about the fire when I saw you at church this morning? I even asked you if something was wrong." As he spoke, he glanced toward the house.

The meaning behind the gesture was clear. He didn't want anyone to see them together.

Erin blinked back the tears that clawed at the back of her eyes and lifted her chin.

"Because it didn't concern you."

Lucas watched Erin's car drive away and resisted the urge to jump in his truck and chase after her. But that would really give people a reason to talk.

The fallout from the bomb his cousins had dropped right before dinner continued to overshadow his thoughts. It was no surprise that someone on Samuel's side of the family wanted to get their hands on the inheritance, but it was the lengths that person was willing to go that concerned him.

He ignored the cold gnawing its way through his shirt as Erin's car turned the corner and disappeared from view.

When Kylie announced that Erin had arrived to

pick up Macy, Lucas had assumed she would come inside to say hello to Kylie and his family. But she hadn't. From the window, Lucas watched her trudge away from the house, a slight figure that didn't look strong enough to withstand a gust of winter wind pushing down from the mountains, let alone some unknown aggressor who might have chosen her café to send out a warning.

But why Erin?

As far as Lucas knew, none of their family or friends knew that he and Erin had secretly dated their senior year of high school.

Lucas frowned as his thoughts turned down another road. It was possible the person who'd been creating the "situations" his cousins had mentioned witnessed the exuberant hug that Max had bestowed upon Erin at the café the day he'd had lunch with Brooke. The affection between them would have been apparent even to a casual observer, making it obvious they had spent time together.

If someone was afraid that Lucas might actually decide to stay in Clayton, a woman with roots in the community as deep as Erin's would be determined a threat.

Whoever was responsible for the attacks against his family didn't want Lucas to have a reason to stick around.

And Erin, Lucas silently admitted, would be a reason.

The first few times their paths had crossed, he'd

blamed the feelings she stirred in him on the memories of a teenage crush. Now he had to wonder if those feelings had never completely died.

Erin hadn't changed. She was still the sweet, kindhearted girl he'd fallen for. The girl who had made him believe there was something in Lucas Clayton worth loving.

But her feelings for him had definitely changed.

Did she blame him for the fire? Or for something else?

Lucas shook that thought away. He'd asked Erin to go away with him and she'd refused. Maybe the spark of anger he'd seen in her eyes wasn't because he'd left but because he'd returned and caused trouble for the people she cared about.

It didn't concern you.

That might be true, but it didn't change the fact that Lucas *was* concerned.

He strode back to the house and realized his absence had created some attention. A trio of little faces tracked his movement like flowers turning toward the sun. He hoped no one else had witnessed his conversation with Erin.

Mei met him in the front hall. "Mom just called. She wants you to stop over for a few minutes."

"Did she say why?" Lucas hadn't seen their mother since Mei had told him that Vern might have had a relationship with Darlene Perry.

"Maybe she just wants to visit with you and Max for a while."

Lucas didn't bother to hide his skepticism. "Maybe."

"Give her a chance," Mei urged. "You aren't the only one who's had to deal with some tough things."

Lucas bristled at the unexpected attack. "I never said I was."

"I want you to think about the fact that maybe it wasn't Grandpa George who brought us back to Clayton."

That might be true, but at the moment, Lucas was more interested in finding out who was trying to get them to leave.

"And Lucas?"

He tried not to sigh. "Yes?"

"Think about it on the way to Mom's house."

Lisette looked surprised when she opened the door and saw Lucas standing on the other side. As if she hadn't believed he would really show up. She tucked Albert, her temperamental Maltese, in the crook of her arm. "Please, come in."

"Hi, Mom." Lucas forced a smile, still not sure he was ready to face his mother in the light of what Mei had told him about their father.

Life had been easier in Georgia, where his emotions could remain safely on autopilot. Lucas wasn't forced to look at Erin Fields and wonder what might have been—or if he'd made the biggest mistake of his life when he'd left her standing in the driveway on graduation night.

He didn't have to drive through a town that kicked

up memories like dust devils, making it difficult to discern the truth from the lies.

"Mei mentioned you wanted to talk to me." Lucas held Max's hand as they followed Lisette into the living room, where a small artificial tree sprouted from the center of the drum table in the corner.

The lights drew Max's eye like a shiny penny in the street. A wide grin split his face.

Lucas might have dismissed it as a hallucination if Max hadn't seen it, too.

"Mei mentioned how excited Max was about her tree the last time you visited, so I thought I should put one up this year." Lisette's smile turned pensive. "It always seemed like a lot of trouble when it was just me."

"Max, no!" Lucas saw the little boy reach for one of the candy canes that decorated the lower branches. "Those are decorations."

"They're also to eat" his mother shocked him by saying. She took one off the tree and handed it to Max. "We can hang another one in its place."

Max hooked the candy inside one pudgy cheek and beamed at her. "Thank you."

Give her a chance, Mei had urged. Lucas took a deep breath. "Mei said you wanted to talk to me," he repeated.

His mother tugged at the strand of matched pearls around her neck. "Mei said the cabin is furnished, but I went through the closets, looking for some odds and ends that I thought you might need."

Lisette gestured toward a cardboard box on the floor next to the sofa. "And I had some things of yours packed away until you…"

You came back.

Lisette didn't say the words out loud, but Lucas heard them anyway. Had she expected he would someday return to Clayton? Had she *wanted* him to come back?

Over time, Lucas had convinced himself that his mother's life would be easier if he simply disappeared. He didn't want to consider that maybe the person whose life had been easier might have been him.

Uncomfortable with the direction his thoughts were taking, Lucas dipped a hand inside the container. The first item he pulled out was a box with tiny silver hinges, handcrafted out of pine.

"I found that on the shelf in your closet." Lisette sat down beside him. "Do you remember it?"

Unfortunately, yes. "Grandpa George gave this to me for Christmas when I was twelve."

"Your father and I weren't sure why your grandfather singled you out that particular year. He had a reputation in the family for being quite the Scrooge."

What Lucas remembered was that his initial excitement over the package that his cantankerous grandfather had handed him quickly faded.

"What's the problem, boy?" Grandpa George had barked. *"You look disappointed."*

Lucas had scraped up the courage to tell him the truth. *"It's a...box."*

An *empty* box, to be exact.

Instead of becoming angry, George's booming laugh rattled the windows. *"I said the exact same thing when my father gave it to me. And I'll tell you what he said. It's a family heirloom. Jim Clayton made that box from a tree that grew on his claim. He built a cabin out of the rest of it. Whoever gets that box gets to decide who to pass it on to. I picked you."*

"Why?" Lucas asked even though he knew the answer. His grandfather would drone on about his good grades or the sports trophies he'd been awarded for basketball that year.

George had poked a thick finger a quarter inch from Lucas's nose. *"Because you, Lucas Clayton, will understand its value."*

Understand it? Lucas had stashed the box in his closet and forgotten about it.

His thumb absently traced the smooth grain of the wood. At the age of twelve, he hadn't appreciated the craftsmanship. Or the history.

"That box is as old as this town," Lisette murmured.

Another unwelcome reminder that his last name bound Lucas to a place he had never felt he belonged.

"I'm still not sure why he gave it to me. Why

didn't he give it to Dad? Or Uncle George?" Some-one worthy of a family heirloom.

"Their relationship was...complicated," his mother said carefully. "George Sr. was a difficult man to please. Much like your father."

Lucas had never heard her say anything negative about his father. She had always been a staunch sup-porter of Vern's rules, no matter how unreasonable. After his death, Lisette had pushed and prodded Lucas to become a doctor.

Lucas opened his mouth, ready to unleash a cut-ting "I didn't think you'd noticed." The two words that came out were, "I tried."

"So did I." Lisette shocked him by saying. "Your father was a gifted physician but he began to rely on himself rather than God. He wanted to do things his own way. When a person becomes proud, it gets easier to pull away from people and more difficult to forgive. Even the people you love."

Lucas stared at the box cradled in his hands.

How many times had he told Erin that he refused to become like his father? What he'd meant was the kind of man whose inner life and outer life didn't match.

Now Lucas realized he was just as guilty of "going his own way." And he'd refused to forgive his father for his harsh demands.

Refused to forgive himself for not making things right before his father died.

He tried to hand the box back to his mother. "You should give it to Mei." His sister had every intention of making Clayton her home once she and Jack were married.

"It's yours." Lisette put it back in the cardboard box. "Maybe Max will like it. Little boys need a place to keep their treasures."

Lucas was too stunned to comment. It was the first time he'd seen any indication that his mother was willing to accept Max into the Clayton family. And the first time since he'd returned to his hometown that he saw a hint of a smile, rather than disapproval, in her eyes.

Maybe Mei was right. Maybe their mother did want things to be better between them.

A loud, staccato thump started at the front door and vibrated through the house.

Lisette rose to her feet. "Excuse me."

She turned a few moments later, Tweed at her side. Lucas automatically rose to his feet at the sight of his boss.

"I saw your truck," the vet said breathlessly, his British accent more pronounced than usual. "A horse trailer slid into the ditch a few miles outside of town and the stallion trapped inside is trying to kick its way out. Come on."

Lucas's pulse spiked. "I have to find someone to watch Max first."

"No!" Max flew across the room and his thin arms came around Lucas's waist like a grappling hook.

Lisette stepped forward. "I can take Max back to the cabin and stay with him until you get home."

Lucas's mouth dropped open. "But—"

"The lady is willing to take a shift," Tweed barked. "Let's go."

Lucas managed to peel Max off his leg. "I'll be home as soon as I can, buddy."

A low whimper was all he got in return.

"We'll be fine, Lucas."

"Are you sure, Mom?" he asked.

"I'm willing to try."

Warmth bloomed in Lucas's chest as he met her uncertain gaze.

Impulsively, he hugged her.

"So am I."

"Is this Erin?"

Erin's hand tightened around the phone as she recognized the breathless voice. "Mrs. Clayton. What can I do for you?"

"I'm sorry to call so late but I'm over at Lucas's. He went out on an emergency call late this afternoon and I offered to stay with Max for a few hours."

Erin glanced at the clock. It was almost ten. She had dropped Macy off at home more than an hour ago and was just getting ready to take a long bubble bath and turn in for the night.

"Is everything okay?" she asked cautiously.

Lucas had hinted that he'd moved out because his mother wasn't used to small children in the house.

Erin had tried not to pass judgment on the woman but Max was such an adorable little boy, she had a difficult time believing that Lisette hadn't immediately fallen in love with him.

The way she had.

"No, it's not." Lisette's voice trembled. "He fell asleep about an hour ago but he just woke up... sobbing. I can't get him to stop and Lucas isn't answering his cell phone."

In the background, Erin could hear a muffled wail. No matter how conflicted her feelings for Lucas, she couldn't turn her back on Max. "I'll be right over."

"Thank you." There was no mistaking the relief in Lisette's voice.

When Erin arrived at the cabin ten minutes later, the door was thrown open before she had an opportunity to knock and Lucas's mother practically yanked her inside.

"He won't stop crying." Lisette, always so put together, appeared completely frazzled.

Hadn't Lucas told his mother about Max's nightmares?

With Lisette at her heels, Erin followed the sound of Max's cries to the small bedroom in the loft. He was huddled beneath the comforter, the heart-wrenching wail punctuated by ragged sobs.

Erin flipped on the switch for the overhead light. The scene that greeted her seemed different from the one she'd witnessed in her living room only a few weeks ago. The terror in Max's eyes had been locked on some unseen horror. Nothing had existed but fear. Now, his eyes tracked her approach, telling Erin that he was aware of his surroundings.

Remembering what Lucas had done, she settled more comfortably against the headboard and drew Max into her arms.

He snuggled closer, resting his head in the cradle of her shoulder. "Do you want to tell me what all these tears are about, cowboy?"

"Lucas is…gone."

Erin nodded. "He had to take care of an injured horse."

"Like Diamond?"

"Uh-huh. And he asked your grandma to stay with you until he got back."

Max's lower lip trembled. "He's…coming back?"

Now Erin understood. It wasn't one of Max's nightmares that held him trapped in the past. This time, it was the future that had him terrified.

"Of course he is," she whispered. "Sometimes he has to go to work but he'll *always* come back."

Max sniffled. "He didn't say goodbye. My dad didn't say goodbye when he left, either."

Lord, give me the right words to say.

"Your dad loved you very much," she said softly. "So much that he asked Lucas, one of his very best friends, to take care of you. Forever. Lucas won't leave you."

"He promised?"

"He promised." Erin's throat tightened. "And Lucas keeps his promises."

No matter that he'd broken the ones he'd made to her, when it came to Max, Erin knew she spoke the truth.

"Can I hava glass of water?"

Erin pressed a kiss against his damp forehead. "Coming right up."

Chapter Thirteen

❧

Erin found Lisette downstairs, standing in front of the stone fireplace, her fingers pressed against her temples.

"Is he all right?"

"I think so. He got scared when he woke up and Lucas wasn't here." Erin suddenly noticed the unshed tears glistening in Lisette's eyes. "Are *you* all right?" she asked tentatively.

"I can feel a migraine coming on," Lucas's mother said. "Do you mind staying until Lucas gets back? My medication is at home and if I don't take it right away, the headache will get worse."

"I'm not sure that's a good idea, Mrs. Clayton—" Especially given the tension between her and Lucas.

"Please," Lisette interrupted. "Kat mentioned the other day how much Max likes you. I'm sure Lucas won't mind."

Erin wasn't sure about that at all. But when she

heard Max call her name, it suddenly didn't matter what Lucas would think. Max needed her.

"All right. I'll stay."

Lucas tried not to panic when he noticed that his mother's car was no longer parked in the driveway.

Had she taken Max back to her house for the night? He had assured her that he wouldn't be gone longer than a few hours but it was close to midnight.

He didn't even take the time to shrug off his coat as he strode inside. "Mom?"

No answer.

The fire cast a bronze glow around the room, illuminating two figures curled up on the sofa.

Max, sound asleep. In Erin's arms.

For a moment, all he could do was stare. Erin's neat ponytail was gone, her hair a fiery cloud around her sleep-flushed cheeks.

"Erin?" He bent down and touched her arm.

She came awake with a start and struggled to sit up. "I'm sorry."

Why did Lucas get the feeling that he should be the one apologizing? Especially because she should have been home, sound asleep in her own bed by now.

Lucas reached for Max. "Stay here. I'll put him back to bed—" his mouth went dry as Erin began to finger-comb the wayward strands of copper hair framing her face "—and you can explain why you're here and my mother is gone."

He gathered Max into his arms and carried him upstairs. The boy's puffy eyelids and tearstained cheeks made his heart sink.

Max stirred as Lucas tucked him into bed. His eyes opened a crack and a sleepy smile lifted the corner of his lips. "Erin said you'd come home."

Home.

Lucas nodded, unable to trust his voice.

"G'night." Max drifted off again, a smile on his face.

He found Erin standing in front of the fireplace. She looked rumpled and worried. And beautiful.

"Max had another nightmare," Lucas guessed. Although why his mother had turned to Erin for help was a mystery.

"It wasn't a nightmare," Erin said slowly. "Not like last time."

Lucas frowned. "Then what was it?"

"When Max woke up and realized you weren't here, he got scared."

Lucas read between the lines. And he didn't have to wonder how his mother had reacted when she'd been unable to console Max. Not when she'd called Erin for backup.

"Your mom felt a migraine coming on and asked if I'd stay until you got back."

"I don't understand." Lucas raked a hand through his hair. "Max was right there when Tweed stopped by my mother's house. He knew I went out on a call."

"He thought you'd left him for good," Erin hesitated. "Like his father."

The color drained from Lucas's face even as his doubts festered. "What was I thinking? I don't know how much longer I can do this," he muttered. "I'm not cut out to be a father. Max should have someone who understands what he needs."

"He needs *you*."

It that were true, it was a terrifying thought. "You make it sound so simple."

"And you try to make it complicated."

Lucas blinked, taken aback by the edge in her voice. He was used to seeing Erin calm. Serene. There was only one other time she'd appeared this ruffled.

Looking at her flushed cheeks and blazing eyes, Lucas suddenly felt as if they'd fallen through a crack in time. The years melted away and they were eighteen again, squaring off against each other like pieces on a chessboard.

"What's that supposed to mean?"

"It means it's late and I'm leaving." Erin's coppery locks got caught in the collar as she struggled to put on her coat. Lucas reached out to help and their hands tangled.

Both of them went still.

They were practically nose to nose. Lucas could see the faint dusting of freckles across her nose. And the weary lines fanning out from her eyes. The faintest hint of smoke clung to her coat.

How could he have forgotten the reason for the weariness that marked her features?

Guilt broadsided Lucas. The last thing he wanted was for Erin to get caught in the crossfire of a feud that didn't involve her.

Unless she got involved with him.

No matter how he felt about her, Lucas couldn't take a chance that whoever had attacked his family would set their sights on Erin.

"I'll do what I think is best," he said.

"Oh, that's right." Erin parked both hands on her hips. "I forgot that *you* get to decide what that is. For everyone." She pivoted away from him.

"You can't make a statement like that and then walk away."

"Watch me."

Erin headed toward the door but Lucas got there first.

He blocked her path. "Tell me why you're so angry."

"How much time do you have?" Erin muttered.

"That does it." He set his back against the door.

She glared up at the underside of his unshaven jaw. "What are you doing?"

"Something we've never had. It's called closure." Lucas folded his arms across his chest.

"I don't *need* closure."

"Dr. Phil would argue that."

Under different circumstances, Erin might have

laughed. She rolled her eyes instead. "It was a long time ago."

"It doesn't *feel* like a long time ago," Lucas snapped.

Erin's pulse sped up. Was it his way of admitting that he still felt the connection between them?

"Lucas—"

"I heard about the things that have been happening to my family over the past few months. I don't want you to become collateral damage because someone thinks we're…involved."

She deserved this for dropping her guard, even for a moment.

"And we can't have that, can we?"

"Why are you angry with me for trying to protect you?" Lucas asked, his voice gritty with frustration.

"I'm angry that after seven years you can't come up with some new material."

Lucas looked shocked. Erin was a little shocked, too, that she'd blurted that out.

"I have no idea what you're talking about."

Erin felt tears sting her eyes. "That was your excuse when we were dating. You didn't want anyone to know about our relationship because you were *protecting* me."

"It wasn't an excuse."

"Sure it was." Erin couldn't stop the words from tumbling out. "Your mother would have loved it if she knew we were dating. You would have done something Lisette might have approved of, and you couldn't have that, could you? Not to mention that you didn't want the kids at school to know you were spending time with sensible, responsible, *boring* Erin Fields."

Lucas's eyes darkened. "That's crazy."

"I'm sorry." Erin marched over to the window to put some distance between them. "Make that sensible, responsible, boring *and* crazy."

"I was protecting your reputation—"

"You were protecting *yours*."

"Where is all this coming from?" Lucas ground out.

"You left!"

"And you *stayed*." Lucas stalked toward her and Erin scooted around the back of the sofa.

"You didn't give me a choice." Erin looked up at the ceiling, as if appealing for help.

"Aren't you forgetting something?"

"No."

"I *proposed* to you," he said gruffly.

"You showed up at my door after midnight, told me you were leaving Clayton for good and asked me to go with you."

"She remembers." He looked at the ceiling, too.

"I remember we argued—"

"*After* you rejected my proposal."

Erin didn't know whether to laugh or cry. "That wasn't a proposal. I would have remembered if there was an, 'Erin, I love you more than life itself.

Will you marry me and make me the happiest man on earth?'"

"You're saying I didn't do it right?"

"I'm saying you didn't do it at all!"

Lucas's lips parted but no sound came out. And then, "It was…implied."

"Implied! It was implied?" Erin's voice cracked. "How do you *imply* a marriage proposal?"

"You should know. You were there." The Clayton dimple made a brief but telling appearance.

Was he actually trying not to smile? Erin was overcome by the urge to hurl a cushion at his handsome face.

And she might have, if his next words hadn't stolen her ability to breathe, let alone move.

"I knew your heart, Erin. Your beliefs. When I showed up at your door that night, I wasn't asking you to go for a cross-country joyride with me. I was asking—in my own bungling way—for you to spend the rest of your life with me."

"No." She rejected the words because to believe them would scrape at a wound that had yet to heal. "You never even looked back. You just…left. There must have been something wrong with me—something that made it easy."

Lucas was silent for a long moment. And then, "Do you remember the first time we talked?"

Remember? The day remained pressed in her memory like a flower.

"You were in detention."

"And Ms. O'Leary saw you in the hall and asked you to keep an eye on the room while she took a phone call."

"You referred to me as 'the warden.'" Erin could still see Lucas in her mind's eye. A blond James Dean in cowboy boots. Long legs stretched out in the aisle. Blue eyes that tracked her every movement below the brim of a battered Stetson that, according to the school handbook, should have been kept in his locker during the school day.

"You weren't the least bit intimidated by me."

"No." Because she'd seen what no one else seemed to be able to see. The grief banked behind the simmering anger in Lucas Clayton's amazing blue eyes.

She'd prayed for him since the night his father and uncle died in a car accident, but they didn't talk. Until that day in seventh-hour detention.

"And I helped you with an English assignment." Erin didn't understand where this side trip down Memory Lane was going to take them any more than she understood the tender look in Lucas's eyes.

"You bullied me into working on my English assignment," he corrected her. "And then I dared you to meet me at the creek that night."

"Only because you didn't think I would."

Lucas had to admit she was right about that. But he'd hoped. Oh, he'd hoped.

Lucas wasn't sure what had stunned him more.

Extending the reckless invitation or the fact that Erin had actually shown up.

He'd waited twenty minutes past the time he'd arranged, mentally chiding himself for sticking around. If he was the poster child for teenage rebellion, God kept a picture of Erin Fields in His wallet. When she wasn't at the library working on her GPA, she was helping her mother at the café.

In detention that day, Lucas couldn't help but be intrigued by her. She didn't call attention to herself the way girls like Susie Tansley did, with heavy makeup and clothes that accentuated their curves. Erin's copper hair hung in a neat braid down her back and she didn't need eyeliner to highlight a pair of big brown eyes a guy could get lost in and never find his way back.

They'd passed each other in the halls, she'd waited on him and his friends at the café, but he hadn't really noticed Erin until that day.

He'd wanted to get to know her better, so he'd tossed out a teasing challenge. His fear that she would show up was equal to his fear that she wouldn't.

Lucas had skipped a rock across the creek, ready to call it a night when a shadow moved through the trees. His heart had done a triple somersault in his chest when Erin came and sat down beside him. Right then and there, he should have known that although Erin Fields might not be trouble according to the population of Clayton, she was trouble for *him*.

They'd talked for two hours. And met the next night. And the next.

Erin had a way of getting to the heart of things—and staked a claim on his in the process.

Now, watching the play of emotions on her beautiful face, Lucas couldn't believe Erin had doubted the depth of his feelings.

He couldn't let her go on thinking that he'd left her behind because of some sort of flaw in her, instead of the ones in him.

"And just so we're clear on this, I was *never* ashamed of you."

"Sure." Erin folded her arms across her chest. "That's why you wanted me to keep our relationship a secret. You could have cleared up the lies Susie told if you'd just been honest about us. That was when I realized that you'd rather let your mother think the worst of you than let people see us together."

The undercurrent of bitterness made him wince. Lucas had convinced himself that breaking off all ties between them had been in Erin's best interests. Now he was beginning to realize how much he had hurt her.

He would have shouted his love for her from the top of Pike's Peak if he'd known what she was thinking.

"Because what we had was...amazing. Special. You know how people like to talk. I didn't want anything to ruin it." Lucas wanted—no, needed—

her to understand. "Your mom was pretty strict and I was afraid that if she knew, she would pressure you to break up with me.

"You were the only person who didn't judge me. Who didn't look horrified when I questioned why God would take two fathers away from their families at the same time." And why He hadn't given Lucas the opportunity to make things right between him and his dad. "When I was with you, I wasn't Lucas Clayton, I was just…Lucas." He sighed heavily. "If I'm guilty of anything, it was being an eighteen-year-old guy who wanted to keep the woman he loved all to himself."

Erin's eyes were huge in her face. For the first time, Lucas had no idea what she was thinking. If she even believed what he was saying.

Maybe it was time to show her instead. And admit that pride—and fear—had played a role in his actions on graduation night. And over the past two weeks while he'd battled his feelings for her.

In one fluid gesture, Lucas vaulted over the sofa and landed next to her. Erin's lips parted in a gasp that turned into a squeak when he reached out to trace the delicate curve of her jaw.

Before she had time to shy away, he drew her into his arms and bent his head, taking her lips in a searching kiss that had nothing to do with the past but hinted at the promise of a future. When Erin's hands looped around his shoulders and skimmed down his back, everything else disappeared.

When they finally broke apart, Erin stared up at him. "That didn't feel like closure," she whispered.

Lucas smiled. "Finally I got something right."

He bent his head and kissed her again.

Chapter Fourteen

Kylie poked her head in the doorway to Erin's office. "Can you come out front for a second?"

The aggravated expression on her friend's face warned Erin that something was wrong. "Sure. What's going on?"

"Billy Dean Harris is at the counter. He insists on talking to you."

Erin released a ragged breath.

Vincent's brother-in-law was the kind of person who liked to "stir the pot" as her mother used to say. Erin closed the computer program she'd been working on and rose to her feet.

Feet that hadn't quite touched the ground since Lucas's unexpected kiss the night before.

Twelve hours later, her lips still felt tingly.

They hadn't had an opportunity to talk because Max appeared at the top of the stairs, wide-eyed and in need of assurance that Lucas hadn't left again.

Which was fine with Erin because she'd been

rendered speechless by that unexpected kiss. A kiss that, amazingly enough, hadn't made her think of the past at all, but opened her eyes to the possibility of a future.

Because they both needed time to think about what had happened—and what it might mean—Erin had gone home, treasuring the memory of Lucas's smile like a keepsake.

He had put to rest the lingering doubts about why he'd kept their relationship a secret.

But he'd still left. And he hadn't made any promises for the future other than the one to his cousins—that he would stay in Clayton for a year.

Lucas might be attracted to her, might still have feelings for her, but it didn't mean he would make the town his permanent home. Or take her with him when he left.

Erin followed Kylie into the dining area. The breakfast rush was over but there'd been a steady stream of customers for the past hour, taking a break from their shopping to get a cup of coffee or hot chocolate.

Billy Dean turned as Erin walked toward him. She was used to him trying to chisel down his bill or get something for free, but the sneer on his grizzled face caught her off guard.

He hooked his thumbs in the grimy suspenders of his bib overalls and glowered at her. "What kind of kitchen you runnin', Erin?" he said without preamble, making no attempt to keep his voice down.

"I ate here yesterday and got sicker than a dog a few hours later. I had to take the rest of the day off from work and stay in bed."

Conversations at the surrounding tables faded, leaving his accusation to echo in the sudden silence.

Erin prayed for patience. "I'm sorry about that, Mr. Harris," she said evenly. "But if you didn't feel well, I'm sure it wasn't from eating at the café."

"Well, Doc Turner thinks different," Billy Dean retorted. "I stopped at the clinic this morning because I still didn't feel right and told him my symptoms. He said it sounded like food poisoning."

Erin's cheeks burned. It was embarrassing that Jonathan Turner might think that something on her menu had made Billy Dean ill. "Even if that's true, I'm sure the meal you had here wasn't the only one you ate yesterday."

"It's the only one that made me sick afterward," Billy Dean roared.

Jerome charged out of the kitchen and skidded up to Billy Dean, slashing a wooden spoon in the air like a fencing sword several inches from the man's bulbous nose.

"I don't know what you're implying, Harris, but on its worst day, my kitchen is cleaner than Marsha's—"

"Now you wait a second, don't you be insulting my wife—" Billy Dean sputtered.

Erin saw an elderly couple exchange concerned looks before they put their coats on and hustled out of the café. "*Please*. Billy Dean. I'd like to offer you a coupon for a free meal—"

A snort followed her offer. "No, thank you, miss. I don't want a free meal *here*. I can't afford to miss another day of work!"

Erin tried not to flinch as the insult hit home.

"Then why stop in and make a fuss?" Jerome hissed.

"Because I thought she'd want to know." Billy Dean's chin jutted forward as he turned to Erin. "Might persuade you to keep a closer eye on things around the place. If business goes down, you might have to shut down."

Erin felt a rush of fear.

Was he trying to warn her? Had Billy Dean set the fire that night? As the husband of Pauley Clayton's daughter, Marsha, he stood to gain a share of George's inheritance if Lucas or one of his cousins didn't abide by the terms of the will.

"Jerome." Erin was surprised her voice sounded normal. "You have some orders to fill. I'll see Billy Dean out."

"I can find my own way well enough." Billy Dean whirled around and stalked out the door.

Erin couldn't help but notice that several other customers followed him. She hoped the timing was coincidental and not a response to the claim that he'd gotten sick from eating at the café.

Kylie, who'd been standing behind the counter

through Billy Dean's tirade, lifted the coffeepot, a question in her eyes.

Erin nodded. "Refills on the house."

Her knees wobbled as she went into the kitchen, where Gerald and Jerome were squared off, crooked nose to crooked nose, in front of the ancient stove.

"...got to tell her," Gerald was saying.

"Tell me what?"

The elderly cooks whirled around.

"Nothing." Jerome's knobby elbow jabbed his brother in the side.

Erin looked at Gerald. "Your ears are red. That means you're hiding something from me."

"Our ma used to say the same thing." Jerome glared at his brother.

Gerald glared back and Erin sighed. "You may as well tell me. I'd rather not get another surprise like the one Billy Dean just delivered."

That seemed to convince them.

"I ran into Dorothy Henry on my way in to work this morning," Gerald said. "Two of her guests at the boarding house complained they didn't feel right after they ate here last night, but I figured Dorothy's chocolate-chip cookies were the culprit. She gives them out at check-in."

"And they sit in a man's stomach like bricks," Jerome felt obligated to add. "Nothing like the ones Arabella makes."

Erin was too dismayed to scold the cook for his

less than flattering description of Dorothy's baking skills. "And she said they got sick from eating at the café?"

Gerald studied the floor. "You know Dorothy. The 'thinking' don't always come before the 'saying.'"

Erin couldn't argue with that. Dorothy Henry was a sweet woman but she also happened to be the biggest gossip in town. Any rumors she started would far outdistance Billy Dean's public announcement by the end of the day.

"No one has ever gotten sick from our food," she said faintly.

"That's a fact," Jerome agreed. "And no one will. Could be a flu bug going around for all we know."

In the cook's flannel-gray eyes, Erin saw both anger and hurt. For Billy Dean to announce to everyone within earshot that he'd gotten food poisoning had the potential to damage more than business. The two cooks prided themselves on their reputation for turning out simple but delicious homestyle meals.

Kylie appeared in the window.

"Order up?" Erin said hopefully.

The waitress shook her head. "Order canceled, I'm afraid. The couple who came in after Billy Dean muttered something about an appointment and left."

Erin tried to smile. "That's all right. Business will pick up over lunchtime."

"Don't worry, Erin." Gerald's liver-spotted hand

clamped down on her shoulder. "Arabella drops off some more of her pies later on and people will be coming down from the mountains to get themselves a piece."

Jerome harrumphed. "Plus we got chicken and dumplings on special today. They'll be standing in line come noon, don't you worry."

Erin lifted her chin. "I'm not worried."

She repeated those words over the next few hours and wondered when she was going to start to believe them.

As the morning wore on and people passed by the window without so much as a glance inside, she silently recited a verse from the Psalms, one that had brought her comfort in the past.

When Kylie walked through the dining room, wiping down the spotlessly clean tables she'd wiped down three times in the past hour, Erin stepped into her path.

"I can cover the rest of the shift, Kylie. I know you have a lot of last-minute wedding details to take care of for Jasmine."

"It's almost twelve o'clock," her friend protested. "What about the lunch crowd?"

Erin scraped up a smile. "I don't think there's going to be one." Or a supper crowd, for that matter.

"This isn't fair." Kylie's indignation matched the furious swipes of her dishcloth against the countertop. "It has to be a coincidence. Think about it—how many bake sales and holiday dinners have taken place over the past few days? There could be tainted meat in a bowl of chili. Sour mayonnaise in a salad."

"Unfortunately, it's a matter of perception, not truth," Erin reminded her. "Billy Dean announced to everyone that Dr. Turner said it sounded like food poisoning. Because he ate here yesterday, the café is suspect."

Kylie looked her right in the eye. "Well, I suspect something—or someone—else."

So, they'd had the same thought. But it was beyond Erin's comprehension that Billy Dean had made up a story in the hope that her business would suffer.

"If Billy Dean was lying, I don't think he would have gone to the doctor. And wouldn't Jonathan have found out when he examined him?"

"Dr. Turner isn't from around here. He doesn't know how crooked the branches are on Samuel's family tree. The whole bunch could have made a fortune on the stage," Kylie pointed out. "And, Erin, we might have to consider the alternative. That someone *did* get food poisoning here."

Erin stared at her friend.

A lie was one thing, outright sabotage another.

"No one would have access to the kitchen. Not with Gerald and Jerome standing guard," she protested. "And I don't think anyone in Samuel's family would stoop that low."

"I know one of them who would," Kylie shot back. "Vincent is a snake. I wouldn't put anything past him."

"Neither would I."

Both women turned at the sound of a familiar voice behind them.

The grim expression on Lucas's face told Erin that he'd been standing there long enough to hear his cousin's name. And he planned to find out why.

Lucas kept his gaze trained on Erin as Kylie grabbed her coat and scooted out the door with a breathless, "I'll leave you two alone. See you tomorrow!"

"What," he asked softly the moment they were alone, "did my cousin do now?"

"Nothing…for sure." Erin caught her lower lip between her teeth.

Lucas's gaze swept the empty tables, pausing to linger on the lone customer sitting near the window and up to the clock on the wall. He had a break between appointments but hadn't wanted to bother Erin, knowing the hours between eleven and one were some of her busiest.

Lucas would have driven past the café if he hadn't felt something. An inner nudge. Now he was glad he had paid attention to it.

He took Erin's hand and tugged her into the office, closing the door behind them.

"Okay. Spill it."

Instead of obeying, Erin began to inch toward her desk.

"If I can scale the sofa, I'm pretty sure that flimsy little desk isn't going to be a challenge."

Erin blushed.

Lucas hadn't meant to remind her of the night before. Even if he hadn't been able to stop thinking about it.

That kiss had lingered in his thoughts through the sleepless night that followed and dogged his trail all morning. The truth was, he'd stopped in because he had to see her again. What he hadn't expected to find was Erin and Kylie Jones in the middle of a conversation about his cousin. He hadn't heard much—just Vincent's name—but it was enough to set off warning bells in his head.

"Billy Dean came in a little while ago and said that he'd gotten sick after eating at the café yesterday."

"He's lying," Lucas said flatly.

"I thought so, too…until Gerald told me that two of Dorothy's guests felt sick last night after eating supper here."

"And Kylie thinks Vincent is responsible." Lucas mentally made the jump from Vincent to his brother-in-law, Billy Dean Harris. It wasn't difficult.

Not with Great-Uncle Samuel's family as close as stepping stones.

"After Kylie broke their engagement, Gabe fired him from the mine. He's been going from job to job ever since."

"So Kylie is the one that Vincent wants to get back at?" he asked.

"I don't know…for sure."

"Please tell me what you *do* know." Lucas had to fight to keep the frustration from creeping into his voice. "Because my family has been leaving a lot of blanks about what's been going on lately."

"Vincent stopped in here last week. He seems to hold you responsible for coming back and jeopardizing his chance to inherit George's estate."

His cousin held him responsible for a lot of things. Other than the broken nose Lucas had given him in retaliation for calling Mei a derogatory name when they were kids, most of the slights had been a figment of Vincent's imagination.

"You overheard him telling someone this?"

"Actually, he told me," Erin said reluctantly. "Somehow, Vincent found out about us. You know how he likes to play mind games with people."

Lucas's back teeth ground together. "He threatened you?"

A shadow crossed Erin's face. "No."

Lucas didn't know if he should believe her. Maybe Vincent hadn't threatened her outright, but whatever he'd said had obviously upset her.

"I'll be back later."

Erin caught up to him at the door. "Where are you going?"

"I think it's about time that I paid my cousin a visit. For old times' sake."

Not knowing which rock to turn over to find his cousin, Lucas made a quick stop at Jones Feed and Supply.

A slow burn had worked its way through him as he remembered the empty tables he'd passed on his way out. First the fire and now an accusation of food poisoning at a time when business at the café would normally be booming.

He'd been avoiding Vincent for two weeks but now Lucas found himself looking forward to seeing the man again.

He threw out a few questions to the cowboys hanging around the coffeepot near the cash register and hopped back in the truck.

Erin was waiting for him on the passenger side.

"I'm coming with you."

Her tone left no room for argument. Lucas almost smiled.

"You have to work."

"I'm the boss. I can take the afternoon off." Her lips curved. "I just had to ask Jerome if that was okay with him."

Lucas's heart tripped over that smile.

He'd kicked himself for crossing a line with Erin.

A line that he'd been responsible for drawing between them in the first place.

Over the course of a sleepless night, he'd tallied the reasons why resuming his relationship with Erin would be a mistake.

He'd come up with an even ten. But with Erin sitting next to him, a smile on her face and a stubborn gleam in her eyes, Lucas couldn't seem to remember a single one of them.

Erin misinterpreted his silence.

"Lucas Clayton, don't you dare tell me that my staying behind is for the best," she warned.

"I wasn't going to."

Because under the circumstances, he figured the best thing to do was keep Erin close.

"Someone saw Vincent turn down Garvey Road about half an hour ago." Lucas put the pickup in gear and backed out of the lot.

Erin's brow furrowed. "The old salvage yard is the only thing on Garvey but Al Hutchins moved away over a year ago. Maybe he hired Vincent to do some plowing or a few odd jobs around the place."

Lucas hoped so. He was tired of Vincent slinking around in the shadows, waiting for the right moment to attack. And he was done letting his cousin use Erin or other members of his family to get to him.

A few miles outside of town, the old farmstead came into view just over a rise.

Erin leaned forward. "That looks like Vincent's

truck." She pointed to the snubbed nose of a black pickup, barely visible between the two outbuildings.

On impulse, Lucas pulled into the cluttered salvage yard, thankful that his reliable but battered truck would blend in with its surroundings. He cut the engine.

Not a minute later, a movement caught his eye. Two men emerged from one of the buildings.

Vincent's muscular frame was unmistakable but it was the other man's hulking form that stripped the air from Lucas's lungs.

Erin was frowning. "There's Vincent but I don't recognize the man with him."

"His name is Maurice."

"You know him?"

"Not personally. The last time I saw him, the police were pushing him into a squad car. He's one of the men who abducted Max."

Chapter Fifteen

Erin stared at him in disbelief.

"But...why is he here? With Vincent?"

"He must have posted bond." Lucas's gaze remained fixed on the two men as they approached Vincent's truck. "When the police picked him up, Maurice claimed he didn't know anything about Scott's murder or a kidnapping. He said he was asked to 'protect' Max during a nasty custody suit."

"Then why follow you to Clayton?"

"I'm not sure if he followed me, or if he was invited." Lucas's jaw tightened. "Vincent wants me out of Clayton. If Max would happen to disappear again, he knows I'll follow."

Everything inside of Erin rebelled against the notion that Vincent was capable of tearing Max away from Lucas and turning him over to the bald, heavily tattooed man whose flat features looked as cold as a mountain spring.

She couldn't suppress a shudder as she imagined

sweet-natured little Max at his mercy. No wonder the boy continued to have nightmares.

"Call Zach," Erin whispered.

"There isn't time for that."

Fear spiked in Erin's throat as Lucas's hand fumbled with the handle on the door. Without thinking, she flung her arm across his broad chest in a futile attempt to hold him in place. "You can't confront them alone."

Lucas tensed, the muscles in his forearm turning to iron beneath her fingers. Erin couldn't physically prevent him from leaving but she hoped that he would realize the danger.

Vincent hopped in his truck and gunned the engine a few times for show. For the first time, Erin noticed the nondescript sedan in its shadow.

As Vincent drove past them, Maurice lifted his nose to the wind like a coyote on a scent trail as he made a slow, thorough sweep of the land before getting into his vehicle.

The sedan started up, the engine settling into a rough purr. A moment later, curls of smoke from a cigarette drifted through a crack in the window.

Lucas's fist smacked the steering wheel.

They couldn't leave without drawing attention to Lucas's truck. Which meant that Vincent had a head start into town.

"Where is Max right now?" Erin whispered.

"With Jasmine." Lucas's throat convulsed, as if he realized the path her thoughts had taken. "Arabella is running errands today so Jasmine is staying home to watch the triplets. They invited Max over to play with them."

Erin opened her purse and began to rummage around for her phone. "I'll call Jasmine and warn her while you let Zach know what's going on."

"So Vincent can worm his way out of this, too?"

"So Zach can *help* you," Erin said. "You don't have to do this alone, Lucas. Zach isn't going to let anything happen to Max, but if you don't do this the right way, someone could get hurt."

She saw the battle going on in the denim-blue eyes before he nodded.

While he dialed Zach's cell, Erin punched in Arabella's number, silently urging Jasmine to pick up. If Lucas was right about Vincent plotting to have Max kidnapped again, then most likely he would be the one to try to sweet talk Jasmine into letting him have Max.

Erin prayed the girl would see through any story that Vincent would concoct to persuade her to release Max into his care. According to Arabella, Jasmine and Cade had been trying to mend fences between their two families for months. Her fiancé didn't approve of his family's behavior, but there was no getting around the fact that Cade was Charley Clayton's son. Vincent wouldn't hesitate to use that relationship if it served his purpose.

"…I'm sure it was him," Lucas was saying in a terse whisper. "I'll meet you at the corner of Waxwing Road in ten minutes. Ask Jack to come with you. He can ID the guy. Maurice was following us the day Jack tracked me to the hotel…right. You, too."

Lucas snapped the phone shut without saying goodbye.

"Jasmine isn't picking up." Erin answered the unspoken question in his eyes.

Lucas's gaze cut from her to the shadowy figure inside the sedan. The butt of a cigarette flew out of the window.

"He's leaving."

Weak with relief, Erin watched the car creep forward and disappear behind the back of the house.

"He's finding a better place to hide." Lucas's fingers trembled as he turned the key in the ignition. "We have to go. Now. It won't take Vincent long to find out where Max is."

"Drop me off at Arabella's on your way to meet up with Zach," Erin said.

"No." Lucas's foot stomped on the gas pedal, causing the tires to buck in the deep snow. "I'm going to drop you off at the café."

"Someone has to be with Jasmine if Vincent shows up at the door."

"I've caused enough trouble for you."

So, they were back to that again.

"I can handle Vincent," she insisted.

"You and whose army?"

"God's."

To Erin's amazement, a smile touched Lucas's lips. "He does seem to look out for you."

"He looks out for you, too," Erin said. "It wasn't a coincidence that you stopped by the café this morning…or that we saw Vincent with Maurice. God takes care of his children."

"His children?" Lucas's lips twisted into a parody of a smile. "You really think He wants to claim me?"

"He already did. And He doesn't let go."

"Jasmine must be home. The lights are on." Lucas pulled up in front of Arabella's house.

"And no sign of Vincent." Erin couldn't hide her relief.

Lucas wasn't ready to celebrate yet. Not when his cousin was making deals with the guy who visited Max in his dreams.

Maurice had left Max in the care of his girlfriend, a flighty twenty-something whose idea of "watching" Max had been to lock him in a closet while she got stoned.

Bile rose in Lucas's throat when he'd watched Vincent thump Maurice on the back as if they were best buddies. He and his cousin had had their differences in the past, but he could hardly fathom that Vincent's hostility and greed ran so deep that he would get involved with a guy like Maurice.

"I'll be back as soon as I touch base with Zach and Jack."

"All right." Erin opened the door and hopped out.

There was so much Lucas wanted to say to her but all he could manage was a grating, "Be careful."

"You, too." Erin flashed a smile over her shoulder.

Lucas watched her auburn ponytail swing between her shoulder blades as she sprinted toward Clayton House.

Heat scratched at the back of his eyes.

God, I don't deserve Your attention, but Erin and Max...keep an eye on them, okay?

It was the first prayer Lucas had uttered in years.

Jack McCord's car was parked on a side street a block from Arabella's. The squad car, with Zach at the wheel, pulled up a moment later.

With Pauley lurking around city hall during the day, they couldn't risk him overhearing their conversation. If Pauley got wind of the fact that his son was in trouble, he wouldn't hesitate to warn him.

Lucas filled them in as quickly as he could, not leaving out Billy Dean's accusation or spotting Vincent's cozy conversation with Maurice.

"I ran Maurice Blanchard," Zach said. "He served time for burglary a few years ago. Crossing state lines is a violation of his parole."

"That will take care of him, but what about Vincent?" Jack put in. "If Blanchard won't talk, Vincent will deny any involvement with him. It will be Lucas and Erin's word against his."

"And we know how well that's worked in the past," Lucas said cynically.

"I have an idea how we can get both of them."

Something in Zach's eyes told Lucas that he wasn't going to like this idea.

"Let's hear it," Jack said, a little too cheerfully under the circumstances as far as Lucas was concerned.

He had to remember this was the guy who'd tracked him and Max down in the Florida everglades, one step ahead of Maurice and his cohorts.

"We have to set a trap for Vincent," Zach said.

But to set a trap, you had to have bait.

Lucas was already shaking his head. "No way. Max and Erin are with Jasmine and the girls. That's putting too many people at risk."

Jack and Zach exchanged looks.

"I called Erin on my way here," Zach said slowly. "She's willing."

Lucas's heart kicked against his ribs. "Willing to do what?"

"Whatever it takes."

Erin glanced in her rearview mirror every few seconds but all she could see was the top of the black Stetson perched on Max's head.

Which meant that Vincent wasn't following them. Yet.

Jasmine had been given instructions that if Vincent showed up, she was to tell him that Erin had picked up Max and taken him home with her for the evening.

Moments earlier, Erin had tried not to let fear overtake her while Lucas stood in tight-lipped silence as Zach laid out his plan.

Now the snow continued to fall as she helped Max out of his booster seat. "We're going out to feed Diamond and then I'll make supper for us."

"Okay," Max chirped.

Her jumbled thoughts tried to form a prayer but Erin gave up. For now, she had to trust that God knew where she was. Knew what she was feeling.

Erin took Max's hand as they walked to the barn, her gaze straying to the access road that ran adjacent to her property. Were Lucas and Jack already there, waiting?

Just the memory of Maurice's cold expression made her knees wobble. Erin would do anything in her power to protect Max from the man who had abducted him but she also knew that her own power wasn't strong enough.

God, protect us. And protect Lucas.

She had no idea what Vincent's latest betrayal would do to a man who'd spent years running from his past. But would Lucas turn away from God again—or run into His arms?

Erin had seen the glimmer of longing in Lucas's eyes when she'd told him that God had claimed him long ago. Like the prodigal son, all he needed to do was come home.

No matter how bad this situation looks, use it for good, Lord.

"I'm gonna see the kittens." Max scampered away while Erin retrieved a piece of straw from the bale near the stall.

"Don't go too far," Erin cautioned, keeping one eye on him as she tossed the hay inside the stall.

The barn, which had always offered a quiet sanctuary to work and to pray, now seemed threatening in the fading afternoon light. Shadows moved on the walls and the creak of the wind through the boards produced a sound that was eerie rather than comforting.

Over Max's giggling, Erin heard a soft thud in the mow above her head. Bits of hay and dust rained down through the cracks.

Zach.

Against Lucas's objections, the deputy had decided that he would be the closest one if Vincent made a move toward Max.

"I'm the only one authorized to arrest a person," Zach had said, reminding Erin how potentially dangerous the situation could be.

"This one likes me!" Max had a round-bellied kitten snuggled in his lap while another batted the laces on his boots.

"I think all of them like you—" Erin's breath stalled in her throat as a low rumble came from inside Diamond's stall. She'd only heard the mare make that sound one other time—when a snake had slithered into the barn.

Erin glanced up. Maybe the mare had sensed Zach's presence.

Max frowned. "Diamond sounds mad."

The sound of the horse's hoof connecting with the wall made both of them jump.

"It's getting dark in here," he whimpered.

"I know, sweetie." Erin bent down and hugged him. "We'll go up to the house now."

Where Lucas and Jack would be waiting.

Maybe they'd been wrong about Vincent. Maybe after talking to Maurice, he'd backed out of whatever plan the two had been concocting.

Please, God.

With one arm around Max's thin shoulders, Erin pushed on the heavy door. The wind whipped in and gave it a yank that almost jerked Erin's shoulder out of its socket.

Max squeaked and wound his arms around her hips.

"It's okay." Erin glanced down to comfort him but Max wasn't looking at her. The hazel eyes had locked on something behind them.

"Who's that?" he whispered.

Relief sifted through Erin, bringing peace to her initial panic. Zach must have come down from the loft. "Your uncle—"

"Yeah, kid. It's your Uncle Vincent."

Erin whirled around, keeping one arm around

Max. Fear turned her mouth to cotton. How had Vincent managed to arrive ahead of them? His pickup had been nowhere in sight when she'd brought Max home with her.

"You scared me half to death." Erin met his gaze without flinching. "What are you doing here?"

Surprise skittered through Vincent's eyes.

Good. Erin didn't want the man to know she was afraid of him. As far as Vincent was concerned, she knew nothing about his meeting with Maurice.

"I got to thinking it's a shame the kid doesn't know the other side of his family." Vincent sauntered toward them, shoulders hunched, thumbs hooked in the belt loops of his jeans. His casual posture belied the sly glint in his eyes. "Thought it was time I did something about that."

"I'm cold, Erin." Max tugged on her sleeve.

Vincent's gaze shifted to the boy and he smiled. "I'm Lucas's cousin. I was hoping you and I could take a ride and see the Christmas lights. Maybe stop for some hot chocolate afterward."

"You're crazy if you think I'm going to let you take Max anywhere." Erin took a step backward and came up against the door. Even if she grabbed Max's hand and tried to make a break for it, Vincent would catch up to them before they made it to the house.

"So protective," Vincent mocked. "But you're not the kid's mother, Erin, anymore than Lucas is your—" He tilted his head. "What's the word they use in those romantic comedies? Oh, I remember now. *Your knight in shining armor.* Those guys are supposed to rescue a damsel in distress, not run off on her."

Erin wet her lips, struggling to maintain her composure. "Lucas had to get out of Clayton," she murmured. Vincent loved to taunt, so all she had to do was keep him talking until help arrived. "It was the right thing to do."

"So noble and self-sacrificing." Vincent shook his head. "And so deluded."

"You're the one who is deluded if you think Lucas is going to let you take Max anywhere."

"I'm doing him a favor." Vincent smirked. "He doesn't want to be tied down with a kid anymore than he wants to be tied down with you. Thanks to his old man, Lucas isn't wired for that.

"He'll spend the rest of his life running. Now me, I stick by my family." Vincent's eyes narrowed. "You and I both know Lucas only came back for the money."

"So you're trying to force him out of town."

"Hey, it worked last time, didn't it?"

It was the opening Erin had been hoping for. "You mean when you convinced Susie to tell everyone she was pregnant with Lucas's baby?"

"She had a thing for him and needed some cash. All I did was come up with a plan so Susie could have both."

"You think you're so smart," she snapped.

"I am. Smart enough to make sure George Sr.'s inheritance goes to the right people."

I hope you're listening, Zach, because it's the closest thing to a confession you're going to get, Erin thought.

Vincent held out his hand. "Come on, kid. Time to see those Christmas lights. And, Erin, don't try to interfere or you'll be waiting tables at someone else's café instead of your own."

"You started the fire," Erin breathed.

"Arson is a crime, Erin." Vincent pressed a hand against his heart in mock affront.

"So is being a party to kidnapping."

Vincent's right eye began to twitch. "I don't know what you're talking about."

"You met with Maurice Blanchard." Erin prayed she wasn't bringing more harm to the situation but she could see that Vincent's patience was wearing thin. Physically, the man outweighed her by about a hundred pounds, all of it muscle. "Zach is arresting him right now."

"You're lying."

"No, I'm not." Erin swallowed hard. "And Maurice is going to turn on you, the same way you turned on Lucas and the rest of the family."

Vincent look undecided for a moment and then his expression turned dangerous. "Give me the kid. Now."

Erin heard the crunch of footsteps on the snowy path leading up to the barn.

A few more seconds…

"He's scared, Vincent. He doesn't know you."

"We'll get to know each other."

Erin lifted her chin. "You'll have to take me with you."

"Now that's the best idea I've heard all day."

Max went limp in Erin's arms as the door of the barn flew open and Maurice Blanchard stalked in.

Chapter Sixteen

Lucas closed his eyes when he heard Blanchard's voice.

What had happened?

Maurice should have been in custody by now. Zach and Jack should be riding in like the cavalry.

Through a crack in the ceiling, he could see Max sheltered in the protective circle of Erin's arms. It took everything he had not to leap down from the loft and take Vincent out. Except now he had Blanchard to deal with, too.

"So, Maurice is under arrest, huh?" Vincent pushed up to Erin. "I knew you were bluffing."

"Lucas—"

"Will thank me for getting rid of both of you," Vincent interrupted. "It'll save him the energy of having to do it himself."

"If you don't think Lucas will try to find Max, then why take him?" Erin pointed out, a note of desperation creeping into her voice.

"Because from what I hear, Lucas has been getting a little too cozy with you lately. We can't have you two playing house, decorating Christmas trees and going to church together. He might forget he's not a family man."

Anticipating Vincent's next move, Erin scooped up Max in her arms. The little boy, who had been silent up until now, began to cry.

"Shut him up while I think," Maurice snarled. "What's going on, Clayton? You said you had a plan."

"And part of that plan was for you to stay put until I brought the kid to you." Vincent stood over Erin, who was trying her best to comfort Max. "I did my part. Now take him and go."

"I like Plan A better." Maurice leered at Erin. "Taking them both."

"Vincent!" Erin shrank back.

His cousin chuckled. "Don't worry—you'll be fine. Maurice is going to tuck you somewhere safe for a while."

Lucas's fist silently pounded his knee. Vincent couldn't be that naive.

Forget the odds. He'd take on both men before he allowed Erin and Max to get into a car with Blanchard.

He scanned the walls for anything he could use as a weapon. Being in the loft put him at a distinct disadvantage. The only way down—a ladder built into the far wall—was in full view of the people clustered near the door.

Erin thought Zach was in the loft but Lucas had talked his cousin into letting him take up position there. He'd needed to be close to Max and Erin if anything went wrong.

And things are going wrong, Lord.

Lucas froze, realizing this was the second time a prayer had slipped out, as naturally as he'd taken his next breath. He tried another.

Erin and Max need Your help. I need Your help.

Below him, Vincent pushed the door open. The motion sensor on the barn flicked on, sending a shaft of light through the loft. Falling on the fire extinguisher attached to a beam on the wall.

Lucas smiled.

He had forgotten that sometimes God's response could be very swift. And extremely practical.

Erin tried to comfort Max as Vincent opened the door and the wind enveloped them in an icy hug.

"Wanna go home!" Max cried.

"I know, baby." Erin's heart threatened to beat right through her chest.

She was not only afraid for herself and Max—she also was afraid for Zach, Jack and Lucas. The bulge in Maurice's coat pocket had the distinct outline of a handgun.

"Wait." Erin tried to appeal to Vincent's conscience one last time. "Max is going to need clothes. And his blanket."

Maurice grabbed her roughly by the arm and gave her a shove. "No more stalling. Hit the lights, Clayton. We're out of here—"

A dull thud followed by Vincent's sudden howl drowned out Max's sobs and Winston's frantic yips.

Vincent crashed to the floor and curled into a fetal position, hands clamped around his head.

Maurice let go of Erin.

"Erin. *Run!*"

Lucas?

Erin didn't wait to find out. She stumbled out of the barn, shielding Max the best she could.

Shadows in the darkness around the barn took on human form as men converged on the scene. Erin recognized Zach as he charged past her, gun drawn.

Jack tackled Maurice before he reached his vehicle.

Oblivious to the cold, Erin sank to the ground, Max still cradled in her aching arms.

The next half an hour was a blur. Zach and a fellow deputy loaded Vincent and Maurice into separate squad cars while a female officer escorted Erin and Max back to the house.

"Would you like a cup of tea?" The officer, a sweet-faced young woman who looked as if she would have been more suited teaching a kindergarten class than police work, offered her a cup of tea. "You look half frozen."

"I c-can g-g-get it." Erin's teeth were chattering as she pushed the words out.

Max had already fallen asleep on the sofa beside her, wrapped in a cocoon of blankets.

"You might want to wait a minute," the officer cautioned. "Zach is doing a...debrief in your kitchen."

"A debrief?"

"With Jack McCord and his cousin, Lucas." Laughter sparkled in her eyes. "But trust me, you don't want to go in there yet..."

Erin was already on her way to the kitchen. She paused in the doorway at the sound of a familiar growl.

"What I want to know is what took you so long?" Lucas was demanding.

"We had to get something on Vincent."

"So we were waiting for the right moment." Jack clapped a hand against Lucas's back.

"Like a fire extinguisher hurtling down from the loft to bean Vincent in the head," Zach said with a weary grin. "Nice aim, by the way. You should consider joining the men's baseball league this summer."

Erin clapped a hand over her mouth but couldn't prevent a weak laugh from slipping through her fingers.

Lucas spun around. "It isn't funny...you're *crying*."

Was she?

Erin pressed her fingertips to her cheeks and felt a jolt of surprise when they came away wet.

In two strides, Lucas was at her side. He swept her against his chest and held her close.

"It's over, Erin. You and Max are safe. It's over." He rocked her in his arms and spoke soft words of encouragement that for some reason made Erin cry even harder.

Jack and Zach looked on in amazement.

"Did you see this coming, Deputy Clayton?" Erin heard Jack whisper.

"No" came Zach's amused response. "It looks like I'm going to have to ask my witnesses a few more questions. Just for the record."

"Someone's here to see you, Erin."

Erin looked up. "The state health inspector?"

Kylie grimaced. "Very funny. No, it's not the health inspector."

Erin pushed away from her desk. She needed a break from the books. After two days, business had been slowly picking up. Very slowly. She had wanted to give her employees a Christmas bonus but now the only thing Erin hoped to give them was their weekly paycheck.

News of Vincent's arrest had swept through the small community, but no one knew the extent of his involvement in the plot to chase Lucas and his cousins out of town. Erin knew the Claytons wanted to keep it that way.

She was glad it was over and they'd found out who was responsible for all the attacks. Maybe now Lucas would finally give himself permission to leave the past where it belonged and embrace the family God had given him.

"Wait! Let me fix your hair."

"Fix my—" Erin batted Kylie's hands away. "What's wrong with my hair?"

"Nothing. Except that it looks like you combed it with a branch from your Christmas tree this morning." Kylie grinned.

Erin paused in front of the mirror. Her neat ponytail had been abused by the constant shuffling of her fingers while she was going over the books.

Kylie plucked at the strings of her apron as she walked toward the door. "You don't need this."

Erin rolled her eyes in exasperation. "Who wants to see me? A celebrity food critic?"

Her friend closed one green eye in a saucy wink. "Better," she whispered.

A split second later, Erin had to agree.

Because Lucas and Max stood by the counter. Both wore jeans, flannel shirts and matching Stetsons on their heads.

A curious lightness began to build in her chest.

"What's going on?"

"A date!" Max shouted.

Now Erin understood. "Oh, you two are having a boys' night out."

Behind the counter, Kylie let out a delicate but audible snort.

"The last I heard—and correct me if I'm wrong—a date involved a guy and a girl," Lucas drawled. "Or on occasion, a guy and a girl and a four year old."

Max nodded happily at having been included.

"You're asking me out on a…date?" Erin ventured, not quite able to believe it. Sure, she'd dreamed about it. Longed for it. But never believed it would ever happen.

Especially given the fact that she hadn't seen Lucas for two days. They'd talked briefly on the phone the evening before but he'd made no move to see her. Until now.

Lucas looked up at the ceiling. "I'm still not getting this stuff right, am I?" Then he turned back to Erin. "Yes, Max and I are taking you out on a date."

"To your house!" Max wasn't about to be left out.

"My place?" Erin echoed.

"And we—" Kylie swept up with a picnic hamper "—supplied the dinner."

Erin's eyes met Lucas's. "I accept."

"Hamburgers and french fries." Max bounced in place, causing the cowboy hat to list over one dark eyebrow.

Erin sent a silent prayer of thanks that he didn't seem to be affected by their harrowing ordeal. It was possible Max hadn't understood exactly what was happening when Maurice showed up at her barn.

She wished she could say the same. Images of the man's leering expression coupled with the drop in business had taken a toll on her peace of mind.

"For Max." Kylie couldn't stop smiling, a proud accomplice to this particular secret. "For you and Lucas, two T-bone steaks, baked potatoes, salad and one of Arabella's famous apple pies."

"Thank you, Jerome and Gerald!" Erin called.

A duet of grunts and coughs followed.

"Go on, get!" Jerome finally hollered back. "You've been puttin' in too many hours as it is."

"Here's your coat." Kylie thrust it at her. "See you tomorrow."

Erin climbed into the pickup next to Lucas and then almost climbed right back out again when she saw the bouquet of red-and-white roses on the seat.

"Those are for you," Max informed her. "Lucas said you haveta give a girl flowers on a date. I'd rather have Legos."

Lucas chuckled. "It's my way of saying thank you. For…everything."

"Thank you." Erin hugged them against her, burying her face in the fragrant petals. "I love them."

I love you. I never stopped.

But gratitude wasn't the same as love. And a date was…a date. It was two people spending the evening together, not a lifetime commitment.

Lucas won't stop running...

Erin pushed Vincent's taunting words aside. He'd already caused enough damage. Tonight she was going to enjoy the company of her two favorite men and not worry about the future.

Max disappeared into the living room to play with Winston moments after they arrived at her house.

Lucas joined her in the kitchen. "You sit down. I've got this."

"Unpacking a picnic basket?"

He responded to her teasing with a smile that made her weak at the knees. "Hey, we all have our talents."

For a moment, Erin enjoyed the sight of Lucas Clayton in her kitchen. *Her* kitchen. She pinched herself under the table, just to make sure she wasn't dreaming.

"How is Max doing?" Not one to remain idle for long, Erin started to put together a tossed salad from the ingredients Kylie had packed in individual containers.

"He took a long nap yesterday afternoon."

"No nightmares?"

"No." Lucas opened the oven and put the steaks under the broiler. "What about you?"

Erin evaded the question. "I still can't believe Vincent was ready to put Max in danger like that."

"None of us can," Lucas admitted. "Zach said Vincent asked for a lawyer right away and he's refusing to talk. But as far as I'm concerned, it's guilt by association. He and Maurice were together. It stands to reason that Vincent was responsible for the attacks on the rest of the family."

"Including the café."

Lucas's expression changed. "It's only been two days, Erin," he said quietly. "Give it some time."

Erin wished she felt as confident. "Vincent won't admit to tampering with the food, so there's no way to prove it wasn't my fault."

"You know it wasn't."

"Yes." But that wasn't what had kept her awake the previous night. "If I ever needed the perfect excuse to close the doors of the café for good, I'm pretty sure this would be it."

Erin couldn't believe she'd actually voiced out loud the thought that continued to plague her.

"Is that what you want?"

"I thought it was. All this time I thought I was keeping Mom's dream alive, honoring something that was important to her…"

"But now it's important to you," Lucas finished.

He had put into words what Erin hadn't been able to.

"A few of my regular customers came in this morning as if they hadn't heard the rumors. When I walked into the kitchen this morning, Jerome and Gerald were wearing Santa hats to cheer me up. The truth is, for years I wanted to be a veterinarian, but now I can't imagine doing anything other than what I'm doing."

"That's funny. The last thing I wanted to be was a veterinarian, and now I can't imagine doing anything else. Thanks to you."

Erin couldn't hide her shock. "To me?"

"For almost a year, I was under the influence of a woman who loved animals," Lucas said. "Some of it rubbed off. The weird thing is, my father would have approved. He claimed that being a doctor was in our blood and since he didn't specify that I had to heal *people*..."

"The family legacy continues," Erin teased.

A troubled frown settled between Lucas's eyebrows before he turned away. "There are some things a man doesn't want to pass on. Look at my father. And Grandpa George. What does it say about a man who has to bribe his family to get them to return to their hometown?"

"It says that it's never too late to change. That he made things right with God and the people he loved."

Lucas opened his mouth but Erin wasn't sure whether he was about to argue or agree with her because Max appeared in the doorway, a wooden camel in each hand.

"I'm hungry!"

"So am I, sweetie." Erin laughed. "We're just waiting for the steaks."

Max's nose wrinkled. "I'd rather have a burger."

"I hope you feel that way when you're sixteen," Lucas said drily. "It'll save on the grocery bill."

Erin drew in a breath.

That didn't sound like a man who was planning to shirk his responsibility. It sounded like a man who was making room for Max in his future.

But would that future be in Georgia? Or a rustic town at the foot of the Rocky Mountains?

That's what Erin was afraid to ask.

Chapter Seventeen

Erin's alarm went off at six the next morning. She fumbled to shut it off, pressed a hand against her forehead and closed her eyes again. A jackhammer pounded against her temples and her stomach pitched like a raft in whitewater rapids.

What on earth?

She'd felt fine when she went to bed that night. She and Lucas had played a game with Max until his eyes could barely stay open. After they'd left, Erin had stayed up another hour reading.

She reached for her cell phone and saw three missed calls from Kylie. Her friend must be anxious to hear all the details of her date with the two most charming men in Clayton. Pushing herself into a sitting position, Erin punched in the number.

"Thank goodness," Kylie said by way of a greeting.

Erin tried not to groan as the words ricocheted

around in her head. "I'm sorry I missed your calls. I guess I overslept. Is everything okay?"

"Zach called me a few minutes ago. Max is in the hospital."

Fear shot through Erin. "What happened?"

"We don't know for sure. He got the news second-hand from Arabella. Jonathan said it sounded like a severe case of food poisoning so Lucas took Max to the emergency room about 2:00 a.m. The pediatrician on call admitted him because they're worried about dehydration."

"Food poisoning." Erin collapsed against the pillow.

It couldn't be. Not again.

"Lucas has a mild case, too," Kylie continued. "But he won't leave Max's side."

"I'm on my way." Erin tried to sit up but it felt as if her stomach stayed in place. She stifled a groan but Kylie heard it.

"Hey, you don't sound too good, either. Are you feeling okay?"

Erin avoided the question. "I don't understand how this could have happened. Lucas and Max were with me last night. We had dinner together."

Kylie was silent as she processed the news. "The dinner we prepared for you—"

"At the café." Erin's breath caught. Everything except dessert. "We had one of Arabella's pies, too. Lucas and I shared a piece but Max ate a whole slice."

"This has got to stop." Kylie's voice shook with emotion.

"But Vincent is in jail." Erin ignored her roiling stomach as she slid from the bed and reached for a pair of jeans. "He couldn't have done it."

"Not Vincent, no," Kylie agreed.

But if he wasn't responsible, then who was? Every member of Samuel's family stood in line to inherit. Marsha and Billy Dean Harris. Charley and Frank Clayton. Even Pauley, the mayor.

As Erin drove to the county hospital a half hour away, she prayed for Max. And for Lucas. The blessing he'd said at dinner made her hopeful that he was back on speaking terms with God. She could tell the prayer hadn't been for Max's benefit but had come from Lucas's heart.

Was his shaky faith strong enough to stand another attack?

Erin made her way to the pediatric unit, pausing to ask a nurse which room Max was in.

"Room 204." A pretty, dark haired nurse pointed to a door at the end of the hall.

Max was alone when Erin slipped into the room. Sound asleep, with his hand tucked against his cheek, he looked even smaller in the hospital bed. His legs moved restlessly beneath the thin blanket.

Erin took his hand and gently traced Max's fingers, careful not to touch the plastic tube in his arm.

A shadow fell over the bed. "How is he doing?" Zach whispered.

"I don't know yet. Lucas isn't here."

"He's around here somewhere. I just talked to him about fifteen minutes ago." Zach exhaled. "He didn't look too good."

"Will you sit with Max for a few minutes?" Erin asked. "I'll find him."

"Sure." Zach caught her lightly by the arm as she took a step toward the door. "This isn't your fault, you know."

He'd talked to Kylie.

"I don't know what else to think." Erin bit her lip. "Vincent was arrested with Maurice. If it wasn't him, then who's responsible?"

"I don't know," Zach said tightly. "But I plan to find out."

Erin walked to the nurses' station and waited until she got the attention of a nurse sitting at the computer.

"Can I help you?"

"I'm looking for Lucas Clayton. His son, Max Cahill, is in a room just down the hall."

"Blond hair? Blue eyes? Cowboy hat?" At Erin's nod, she pointed to a small hallway on the right. "I think he's in the chapel."

"Thank you." Erin had seen the small gold sign on the door as she'd walked off the elevator.

The door was closed. Gathering up her courage, Erin turned the knob.

"If you don't mind, I'd like to be alone."

Erin stopped. The sight of Lucas, sitting on the

bottom step of the small altar, his shoulders set in a rigid line, fractured her heart. The night before, he had laughed with her. Challenged her and Max to a french-fry-eating contest. As the evening wore on, Erin didn't even feel as if she and Lucas were settling back into their old relationship. This had felt different. New.

Better.

Now she could see that any ground they'd gained was gone. But Erin wasn't going to give in without a fight.

Lucas held his breath, waiting for the door to close behind her. He couldn't face Erin. Not now, when the softest glance or slightest touch would cause him to crumble.

Over and over, his mind played through the past six hours. Watching Max doubled over, his eyes glazed with pain, had been worse than waiting out one of his nightmares.

Lucas, so calm and efficient on the job, had felt totally helpless in the face of the boy's misery. He'd wanted to break down and cry right along with him.

The early hours of the morning blurred together. Lucas had called Jonathan and woke him out of a sound sleep. The doctor had listened to Max's symptoms and suggested that Lucas take him straight to the hospital to find out what they were dealing with. The clinic he'd opened in Clayton wasn't equipped to handle cases like the ones Lucas had described.

The pediatrician had admitted Max immediately. Lucas called his sister and asked her to get a message to Tweed that he wouldn't be at work that day.

Mei must have called the rest of the family to let them know what had happened...

He snapped back to the present when the door closed, snuffing out the light from the hall.

For a moment, Lucas thought Erin had left. Until she sat down beside him.

This was the reason he hadn't called her to tell her that Max was in the hospital. It would be more difficult to stick to his decision while looking into Erin's compassionate brown eyes.

So he just wouldn't look at her.

"I'm going to call Mark Arrington, George's attorney. There has to be a loophole in that will. If he can't find one, I'll find a way to come up with my share of the inheritance and divide it among them." Lucas had already thought it through. He had some money saved, and the rest he might be able to borrow.

"Your family wants you to stay—and not because of the money or the land," Erin said evenly. "Your grandfather's will wasn't to divide his assets. It was meant to bring his family back together."

"Tell that to Samuel," Lucas said bitterly.

"You'll hurt your family more if you leave."

He refused to back down. "I'm not going to stay here and put everyone at risk."

"Or yourself," Erin said softly.

"What's that supposed to mean?"

"If you walk away, you're in control. If you stay, you might have to change." Her knuckles rapped the top of his Stetson. "No more Lone Ranger. You'll have to open up your life and your heart to the people you care about."

And disappoint them?

No, thanks.

Lucas still hadn't recovered from the image of Max's accusing eyes when he'd bundled him into the pickup and driven him to the hospital. It was bad enough to know that he couldn't take the pain away. Worse to know that in a sense, he was the one who'd caused it.

"You don't understand."

"That's where you're wrong. I know what it's like to have expectations placed on you. What it's like to lose a parent. I even know what it's like to have life take an...unexpected turn." Erin linked her fingers through his. "God understands, too. That's why He promised that no matter what we go through, He never leaves us or forsakes us."

Lucas stared at Erin.

Until this instant, he had never realized how closely their lives paralleled each other. The difference lay in how they had handled the things that had come their way.

From the moment Erin had walked into detention that day in high school, Lucas had been drawn to the peace in her eyes while refusing to recognize its source. Faith. Erin had clung to hers while Lucas had walked away from his.

And he'd been lost ever since.

Maybe Brooke had been right when she'd said that it was God—not Grandpa George—who had brought them all home.

Brought *him* home.

Lord, if You've been waiting all this time for me to come to my senses, thank You. I'm tired of doing things my own way. Your plan, whatever it is, has to be better than mine. Mine's taken me on a path to nowhere.

He let out a slow breath as the weight in his chest lifted. And then it disappeared completely. Erin had been right. New *was* better.

"I should check on Max." Maybe he hadn't been a good son, but with God's help, he just might be a good father.

Lucas rose to his feet. "Are you coming with me?"

"Do you want me to?"

Lucas could have kicked himself when he saw uncertainty flicker through Erin's eyes. He was responsible for her doubting herself. And his feelings.

He vowed to make it up to her somehow. He nodded.

As they walked down the hall to Max's room, Lucas glanced through the doorway of the waiting room.

And stopped so abruptly Erin was three steps ahead of him before she realized he'd stopped moving.

The family lounge was crowded with…family. *His* family.

Not only Lisette, but Mei and Jack. Brooke and Gabe were pouring cups of coffee. Kylie and Zach had taken their place by the telephone. Arabella and Jonathan. Vivienne and Cody. Even Jasmine and Cade were there.

Zach wore his uniform and Jonathan was in a pair of rumpled scrubs. Cody and Cade looked as if they were fresh off a cattle drive. It was clear that everyone had dropped what they were doing to make the drive to the hospital.

Erin had been right about that, too.

The doctor stopped just inside the doorway. "Mr. Clayton? If you'd step out into the hall with me for a moment."

"That's all right, Dr. Platt. Whatever you have to say, you can say it in front of my family."

Erin's hand tightened in his.

"All right," the pediatrician said briskly. "The initial tests for E. coli and salmonella came back negative. The lab is checking for a few other things, but Max is resting comfortably now."

Lucas and Erin exchanged looks. "What does that mean?"

Dr. Platt smiled. "It means he can go home as soon as he keeps some fluids down. Which should be in a few hours."

"Thank you, Doctor." Lucas stretched out his hand and the doctor shook it.

"Go on." Arabella motioned toward the door. "We're not going anywhere."

Lisette took Lucas's face in her hands and pressed a kiss smack dab in the middle of his forehead, the way she had when he was Max's age. "We'll be here when you get back."

There was a commotion in the hallway as he and Erin made their way back to Max's room. A nurse went scurrying into one of the rooms but it was Erin's soft gasp that pushed him into high gear.

Erin was a step behind Lucas as he rounded the doorway into Max's room.

"I'm sorry, Mr. Clayton." The dark haired nurse raised her voice a notch above the muffled sobs from the boy thrashing around beneath the thin white blanket. "A minute ago he was sound asleep."

Lucas sat on the edge of the mattress. "Hey, cowboy," he murmured.

"Daddy!" Max wailed.

Lucas's heart plummeted, because he knew Max had asked for the one thing he was unable to give him.

But there was one thing he could—the same thing he'd done the last time Max had been caught in a nightmare. And the time before that. He wrapped his arms around the thin frame and settled him against his chest.

"Da—" a long shudder "—ddy."

Lucas held on tight. His eyes met Erin's over

Max's head to see if she was praying. Unshed tears glistened in her eyes and she was…smiling.

Smiling.

The mattress dipped as Erin sat down on Max's other side and stroked his damp hair away from his cheek. They sat that way for the next half hour, linked together by the little boy in the center of the bed.

When Max finally fell back to sleep, they slipped out into the hall. The minute the door closed behind them, Lucas leaned against the wall and closed his eyes.

"He's going to be okay, Lucas," Erin said.

"Physically, yes." Lucas pushed away from the wall and shoved his hands into his pockets. "I thought…he hasn't had a nightmare in days. I thought he was healing."

"He is healing."

"You heard Max. He was calling for his dad."

"Yes, he was."

"Then how can you say that?"

Erin slipped her arms around his waist and tipped her head to look at him. "Don't you understand? He was calling for *you*, Lucas."

"We have a plan," Brooke announced the moment they returned to the family lounge. "And it's a good one."

"That's what Zach said a few days ago." Lucas scowled at the deputy sheriff.

"I'm in," Erin said promptly.

"You don't know what it is yet," Lucas muttered.

"Whatever it is, it has to better than the one you came up with."

"Let me guess," Mei said. "Did his plan involve a suitcase?"

"That was Plan A," Lucas admitted with a sideways look at Erin. "Plan B is staying put for a while."

For a while.

Erin tried not to read too much into the words.

"Vincent isn't talking," Zach said. "So it's up to us to figure out who's willing to go to such desperate measures to get us to leave Clayton."

"And how do we do that?" Lucas looked skeptical.

"We make it easy for them," Jack drawled.

Chapter Eighteen

"It's almost time." Erin drew in a ragged breath, her chest as tight as the knot in her apron. "Is everyone here?"

Kylie nodded. "I think so. Lucas just drove up."

The knot tightened.

Erin hadn't spoken to him since Max was released from the hospital the day before, but she hadn't stopped praying that Lucas had reached a turning point in his relationship with God. And his family.

She could tell he'd been touched by the fact that no one had budged from the waiting room until Max was released from the hospital later in the afternoon.

Oddly enough, Erin was the one who'd felt out of place. No one questioned her right to be at the hospital, but the curious glances cast her way let Erin know that everyone was wondering what—if anything—was going on between her and Lucas.

They weren't the only ones.

"Sorry I'm late." Lucas shucked off his coat as he walked through the door. "I had to play a quick game of Candy Land with Max and my mom before I left."

"Quick?" Arabella laughed. "That game can last all day."

"I should have remembered that before I agreed" came the wry response. "Erin and I played two games with him the other night. I've performed surgeries that didn't take as long."

Once again, Erin felt the weight of those curious eyes upon her.

Zach came to her rescue.

"Arabella is going to give each of us a job," he said. "We have two hours until we meet up with Reverend West for Christmas caroling."

Each of them had a job to do—and a part to play—in their plan to catch a criminal.

Kylie had taken advantage of her six-hour shift to tell anyone who would listen how excited she was that all the Claytons were going to meet at the Cowboy Café that evening to prepare the food for Jasmine and Cade's reception dinner. Zach was confident the local grapevine would take it from there.

After Erin closed up for the day, Arabella and Vivienne had hauled in their state-of-the-art baking supplies and cookware to boost Jerome and Gerald's meager supply.

"Everyone smile for the camera," Jack said.

Erin appreciated the man's attempt to lighten the moment but the reminder that they'd met for more than a social get-together weighed heavy on everyone's mind. Zach had hidden two video recorders inside the café. One in the kitchen and one in the dining room.

Everyone had been willing to put their own schedules on hold for the moment. If Zach's plan didn't work, then another case of food poisoning would be attributed to the café and more attempts would be made to "persuade" the Claytons to leave town.

Arabella stepped forward. "I think we should start with prayer."

As if by silent agreement, everyone gathered in a circle.

One by one, everyone spoke a few simple words, straight from the heart.

There was a moment of silence after Erin finished praying. And then it was Lucas's turn. For a second, she thought he would pass. Even though she'd sensed that he was on speaking terms with the Lord again, it was another thing to speak to Him out loud, with his family listening.

"Lord." Lucas's husky voice seemed to catch on the word. "Thank You for bringing us together tonight. Thank You for…family. But most of all, thank You for loving us no matter what. Amen."

A familiar, tinkling laugh followed Lucas's quiet benediction.

"Well, look at this! For a second, I thought I accidentally walked into church instead of the Cowboy Café."

"Mom." Arabella twisted her hands together as Kat sauntered in. "I didn't expect to see you here."

"I suppose that's because no one remembered to invite me." Kat shed a red leather coat a shade lighter than her hair and tossed it over the back of a chair, a good indication that she intended to stay.

"Jasmine said that she and Cade were babysitting my granddaughters tonight because all the Claytons were meeting at the café to make food for the reception. And since I'm a Clayton…" Her green-eyed gaze swept the faces of the people gathered in the kitchen, almost as if she were waiting for someone to challenge the statement.

"That's great," Vivienne said with forced cheerfulness. "We need all the help we can get."

Kat patted her niece's cheek. "Of course you do, dear. Now, what can I do?"

"There's a box of petit fours on the table." Arabella stepped in and pointed to one of the tables. "You can attach a frosting rose to the top of each one."

Erin hid a smile. Arabella had put her own mother in the corner to keep her out of trouble.

Brooke, Mei and Kylie sat together, putting together sprays of colorful silk flowers and greenery to form centerpieces for the reception tables.

Under the supervision of Arabella, Vivienne and Erin, the men filed into the kitchen to help with food preparation.

"Jasmine and Cade wanted a fun reception with a Western theme, so we're going with chicken and ribs and all the fixings," Erin said.

"And the best part is, we get to sample as we go," Cody said with a grin.

The men pitched in like troupers, their banter dispelling the tension that continued to mount as the evening wore on.

"This is going to work," she heard Zach tell Lucas at one point. "We'll find out who's been causing all this trouble and then all you have to do is finish out the year."

Erin left the kitchen, afraid to hear Lucas's response.

Erin was avoiding him.

Lucas tried to catch her eye several times over the course of the evening but she flitted from person to person like a butterfly, never staying in one place for more than a few minutes.

Smiling at everyone but him.

Lucas wasn't sure what had caused the change in Erin, but he knew they needed some time to sort things out. Alone.

"Erin? I think Lucas needs a lesson in making gravy," Kylie sang out.

Lucas pretended to be offended. "What's wrong with adding some texture?"

Erin left her station to examine the contents bubbling in the pot. "See this wire whisk? It's your new best friend."

She would have moved on, but Lucas caught her arm. "Max wants to see you."

That earned a smile. "How is he doing?"

"Feeling well enough to beg for a candy cane off Mom's tree," Lucas told her.

A faint smile touched Erin's lips. "I'm glad he's feeling better."

Lucas was aware of the looks and smiles being exchanged between the kitchen crew.

Was I thanking You yesterday for my family, God? Because right now I could use a few minutes alone with Erin...

A tap on the window drew everyone's attention.

"That's our cue," Vivienne said.

Lucas saw Reverend West, his wife, Laura, and several members of the congregation waiting for them on the sidewalk.

"And just in time." Cody sighed. "Those little frosting roses were staining my fingers *pink*. A guy has a reputation to uphold, you know."

Vivienne batted her eyelashes. "Don't worry, honey. With that five o'clock shadow, you still look like a tough cattle wrestler."

"Wrangler." Cody heaved a sigh. "The word

is *wrangler.* What did New York City do to you, sweetheart?"

"It made me appreciate Clayton, Colorado, even more." She gave him a radiant smile.

"I can't remember the last time I did this," Lucas muttered as he shrugged his coat on.

"I do," Mei said. "But you weren't singing with the carolers. If I remember correctly, you were caught *pelting* them with snowballs."

She was right.

"I didn't stay away long enough," Lucas complained. "You still remember all of my stupid mistakes."

"Not all of them." Vivienne sashayed past, knotting a colorful scarf around her neck.

"She's right." Zach thumped him on the back. "There's waaay too many."

"But the past is in the past. And we love you." Mei linked her arm through his.

Lucas felt his throat tighten.

Maybe his family was willing to forgive him, but he had a lot to make up for.

Starting with the slender redhead who had managed to slip out the door when he wasn't looking.

A half a block from the café, Erin realized she'd left her mittens in her office.

"I'll be right back," she whispered to Kylie as the carolers crossed the street.

"Hold on." Someone snagged her arm. "If I can't sneak away, neither can you."

Erin felt Lucas's touch all the way to her toes. "I forgot my mittens," she said. "I'll be right back."

"Do you want me to come with you?"

"No." *Yes.* "I'll catch up in five minutes." Erin didn't give Lucas a chance to argue. With a quick smile, she broke free and jogged down the sidewalk toward the diner.

She skirted around the back of the building and unlocked the door. All the lights were off, but the mouth-watering scent of BBQ lingered in the air.

Erin was about to enter her office when she heard a noise. Her heart jumped into her throat.

As far as she knew, everyone in their group was still caroling with Reverend West.

She took a few careful steps toward the kitchen, listening intently even as she scolded herself for having an overactive imagination. There was no way Samuel or one of his cohorts would choose to break into the café now. Not with the other side of the Clayton family gathered a block away, singing around the Christmas tree in the town green.

It's an old, creaky building, Erin told herself.

The confrontation with Vincent and Maurice had her spooked, that was all. But it still didn't prevent a cold shiver from racing down Erin's spine as she heard the noise again.

She peeked around the doorway and her knees went weak with relief.

Kat Clayton stood in front of the row of pies, still warm from the ovens. Erin wasn't that surprised to see her, given the fact the woman had turned up her nose at the idea of caroling. Kat had started out with the group and must have doubled back at some point to take shelter from the cold.

But Erin couldn't let the woman's presence mess up the trap that Lucas's family had gone to such lengths to set, either.

"Kat?"

Kat jumped a foot in the air and dropped whatever she was holding onto the floor. It spun out of her hand and stopped at Erin's feet.

"What are you doing here?" Kat squawked.

"I forgot something." Erin automatically bent down to retrieve the object Lucas's aunt had dropped.

"Leave that alone." Kat charged toward her, her face twisting with something akin to panic.

"What…" Erin's mouth dried up as she stared at the tiny glass medicine dropper in her palm. "What is this?"

Kat's nostrils flared. "It's mine, if you must know. My medicine."

Erin looked at the clear liquid in the dropper. And then at the food they'd spent the last few hours preparing. "You put something in the food."

"Don't be ridiculous." Kat drew herself up and glared at Erin. "Why would I do that?"

"Because you don't want Jasmine and Cade to

get married." It was beginning to make sense. Jasmine's wedding dress. Everyone had assumed one of Samuel's relatives was responsible, but to cause trouble in Lucas's family, who better than a member of that family?

"You are so naive." Kat's shrill cackle echoed through the empty diner. "I don't care about the wedding. Although, I could buy them a nice gift with the money I earned. Especially now that we don't have to split it with Vincent."

The money she'd earned?

Erin took a step back and slipped the dropper in her pocket, unnerved by the almost gleeful expression on the woman's face. "You were helping Vincent."

"Helping him?" Kat snorted. "Vincent is all muscle and no brains. He was helping *me*."

"But…you're Arabella's mother."

"Thank you for the reminder" came the cutting response. "But I don't owe my darling daughter a thing. Arabella made her choice to stay in Clayton. Just like you did." She shrugged. "A woman has to do what a woman has to do."

And this woman had definitely come unhinged.

"You put poison in people's food!" Erin remembered Max lying in the hospital bed, so small and fragile, and felt physically ill. "You're crazy."

"Like a fox." Kat winked at her as the front door opened and a familiar voice called her name.

Lucas.

Thank You, God.

Before she could open her mouth, Kat beat her to it.

"We're in the kitchen, Lucas," she wailed. "Please, hurry!"

Lucas rounded the corner at a run, his gaze sweeping over the room and settling on Erin.

Kat latched on to his arm. "I came back to get my purse and caught Erin putting something in the food."

Chapter Nineteen

Erin stared at Lucas's aunt, dumbfounded.

"That's not true." Her voice barely broke above a whisper.

"Check her coat pocket if you don't believe me," Katrina cried. "I saw her hide the vial when I came in."

"What's going on?" Zach appeared in the doorway, flanked by Jack and Cody. The rest of the Claytons crowded in behind them.

Erin didn't get an opportunity to speak as Kat appealed to her other nephew now. "Arrest her, Zachary. She's the one who has been causing all the trouble. She and Vincent deserve to sit in jail together."

Erin felt as if she were living one of Max's nightmares. She turned to Zach. "Kat is lying. She teamed up with Vincent. She admitted it a few minutes before Lucas came in."

Arabella's gasp drew Kat's attention. "She's trying to frame me, sweetheart. Can't you see that? Samuel and Vincent promised her a cut of the inheritance."

"Why would Erin do that, Mom?" Arabella's voice shook.

"Revenge," Kat said without missing a beat. "Erin never forgave Lucas for walking out on her seven years ago. He made her all kinds of promises he didn't keep."

The cousins exchanged looks.

"Is that true, Erin?" Zach asked. "You and Lucas were dating and he broke up with you?"

She nodded before Lucas could say anything.

A triumphant gleam appeared in Kat's eyes. "Check her pocket," she demanded. "You'll see that I'm the one telling the truth."

Zach didn't move. Erin withdrew the dropper from her pocket and handed it to him.

Silence descended on the room.

The way Kat had neatly turned the tables on Erin had sent her reeling. She wasn't even sure what she could say in her defense.

To her absolute astonishment, Lucas slipped his arm around her shoulders.

"Erin isn't that kind of person. She would never hurt anyone. Not for money. Not for *any* reason."

The quiet confidence in his voice gave Erin

strength. If Lucas believed her, maybe the others would, too.

"He's right." Arabella faced her mother. "But you would."

Katrina, in a performance worthy of an Academy award, pressed a hand against her heart. "You're my daughter. How can you accuse me of that?"

Arabella shook her head. "That's why you came back," she said slowly. "Not to reconnect with your family. You want the same thing as Samuel. The money and the land. And this proves you were willing to do anything to get it."

"She's the one holding the vial. It's my word against hers." Kat cast a malevolent look at Erin.

"No, it isn't." Zach raked a hand through his hair, his expression weary rather than victorious.

Cade pointed to the clock.

"Smile for the camera, Aunt Kat."

Her features contorted into a mask of rage and accusation. "You set me up!"

"You set yourself up," Zach said evenly. "Samuel and Vincent were using you—"

"Using me?" Kat sneered. "Oh, please. I was using *them*. My father taught me all about blackmail and payoffs. Ask Darlene Perry if you don't believe me."

"You can explain everything," Zach said. "In the police report."

"I've got nothing to say to you." Kat tossed her

head. "You're just as guilty as I am. None of you came back here to reconnect with your roots."

"Not at first," Brooke murmured.

"You're as bad as her." Kat pointed at Arabella. "I don't need a sermon. I need the money that should have been mine to begin with. But no, my father, the man who'd been controlling and self-centered all of his life, had to perform this great noble act before he died. I don't know what he hoped to accomplish."

"He wanted to change things." Vivienne stared at her aunt as if she'd never seen her before.

Mei linked her arm through Arabella's in a show of solidarity. "He *did* change things."

Kat's lips twisted in disgust. "You're all weak. Every one of you. I'd rather sit in jail than listen to this."

Jonathan wrapped Arabella in a protective embrace as she fought to hold the tears back.

"I can take care of that." Zach took his aunt by the arm and began to lead her away. "Erin?" He paused as he reached the doorway. "I'm going to need that vial. And I'll need a statement from you, too."

The stress from the past ten minutes had left her feeling a little shaky. All Erin could manage was a brief nod.

"I'll walk with you over to the station," Lucas said.

"No." Erin carefully extricated herself from the warm refuge of his arms. "Your family needs you right now."

"Don't worry. We'll clean up." Kylie wrapped Erin in a tight hug. "I'll lock up here when we're done."

"We'll have to throw away all this food now," Vivienne said in a low voice. "What are we going to do?"

Arabella summoned a shaky smile.

"We're going to give them a wedding to remember."

"Whatcha doin'?"

Lucas felt a tug on his leg. Max had joined him at the window, where he'd been staring at the smoke curling from Erin's chimney for the past fifteen minutes. She hadn't returned his phone calls that morning, but when he'd called the café, Kylie said that Erin hadn't come in to work yet.

"Thinking," Lucas said truthfully.

"Okay." Max pursed his lips together and frowned in what Lucas realized was a parody of his own expression. "I think we should go to Erin's house."

"You know something, Max?" Lucas grinned. "You read my mind."

He was anxious to talk to Erin. She'd looked shaken by Kat's accusation...and even more surprised that he hadn't believed Kat's lies.

It was becoming clear that Erin still harbored doubts. Not about him—about herself.

That blew him away. How could she not see

what everyone else saw in her? The perfect blend of sweetness and spunk.

The perfect woman for him.

Lights shone in the windows of the barn so Lucas parked outside the door and helped Max out of the truck.

Frank Clayton's gelding poked its nose out of the stall, the velvet lips tugging at Lucas's sleeve when he paused to say hello.

In the chaos of the past few days, he had forgotten about the horse. But Erin hadn't. The door next to Diamond's stall sported a red velvet bow.

"I'm gonna find the kittens." Max broke away from him, not the least bit hesitant to revisit the place where the man from his nightmare had come to life again.

Lucas had Erin to thank for that, too. Sometime in the past twenty-four hours she had transformed the barn into a wonderland of twinkling lights. They were everywhere. Tacked along the walls. Fashioned into the shape of a star above the bales of hay where the kittens played.

Erin didn't want Max to remember the darkness. She wanted him to laugh and play and feel safe, surrounded by lights.

The barn looked a lot different than it had a few nights ago, when he'd been lying on his belly in the loft, listening to his cousin coolly transfer Erin and Max into Maurice's keeping.

And the woman who had willingly put herself in

danger for his son was singing along with a familiar Christmas carol, her lilting voice joining the chorus in a stirring rendition of "Emmanuel" that vibrated the speakers of a dusty radio plugged into the wall.

God with us.

Lucas could finally accept that as truth.

Thank You.

Talking to God was getting easier, too. Maybe, Lucas thought ruefully, because the last few days had given him ample opportunity for practice.

Erin's solo abruptly stopped as Max dashed past her, chasing after one of the kittens. A second later, she peeked around the corner of the empty stall.

Lucas's heart crashed into his rib cage, a familiar response whenever he saw Erin. "Hi."

Very smooth, Clayton. Maybe you should stick to charming horses.

"Hi." She blew a few strands of copper hair off her forehead and smiled down at Max. "Hey, cowboy. You're up bright and early."

"That's 'cause I gotta secret."

Erin looked at Lucas but he appeared as mystified by Max's announcement as she was. She went down on one knee, bringing them to eye level.

"A secret? That sounds serious."

Max nodded, as if he expected Erin would understand.

After everything that had happened, Lucas didn't

appear quite so understanding. "Who told you a secret, Max?" he demanded.

Max's eyes went wide at his tone. "M-Macy did."

"Macy?"

"Uh-huh." Max scraped the toe of his boot against the floor. "She wants a kitten for Christmas."

Erin looked at Lucas and saw her relief mirrored in the blue eyes. "A kitten."

Max pursed his lips. "It's okay that I told, isn't it? 'Cause how is she gonna get a kitten if you don't give her one?"

"Mmm. That's a good question." Erin rocked back on her heels. "You did the right thing."

"So we can give her one?"

Erin hesitated. It was only a matter of time before Macy moved in with Brooke Clayton. She didn't want to cause trouble if Lucas's cousin didn't want a furry livewire in her home, but she didn't want to pass up the chance to brighten Macy's Christmas, either.

"What do you think?" Lucas asked.

"I think Macy must like Max an awful lot if she's willing to tell him a secret." Erin stood up and brushed her hands off. "So, I say we make Macy's Christmas wish come true. Would you like to pick one out, Max?"

"I know which one!" Max dropped to his knees in the swarm of kittens and picked one up, draping it over his arm like a furry purse. Instead of trying to scramble away, the calico closed its eyes and began to purr, its soft paws kneading the sleeve of his coat.

The perfect choice for a ten-year-old girl.

"I'm sure she'll love this one," Erin said in a husky voice.

Max beamed. "Let's go."

"Right now?" Erin slanted a look at Lucas. Under the circumstances, she didn't know if they should show up at Macy's house unannounced. "I received a prayer request this morning about Darlene."

Lucas understood. "I did, too. Maybe it would lift Macy's spirits if we stopped over and surprised her," he said quietly.

"It will." Max snuggled the animal. "Can I have one, too, Daddy?"

"That's up to Erin."

Erin's gaze shifted from the sparkle in Max's eyes to the tender look in Lucas's and knew at that moment, there wasn't anything he wouldn't give the boy to put a smile like that on his face.

She might as well use it to her advantage.

"Butterscotch has six kittens. I think I can part with one. Or two."

Max's face lit up. "Two?"

"You're going to pay for that," Lucas whispered in her ear.

"Mmm." Erin tipped her head. "Think of it as *payback* for the horse in the stall behind you, Dr. Clayton."

* * *

Max sang to the kitten in its carrier on the way out to Darlene Perry's. Erin stared out the window and Lucas knew she was thinking about how difficult the coming days would be for Macy.

"She has family."

Lucas was just beginning to understand the value of those words.

"I know." Erin gave him a tremulous smile. "I was remembering how hard it was when Mom died. She was sick for a long time, too."

And he should have been there for her.

It would take Lucas a lifetime to make up for the last seven years—but he was looking forward to it.

Jonathan Turner greeted them at the door. He'd exchanged his shirt and tie for jeans and a cream-colored fisherman's sweater but there was no doubt he was the acting physician.

"Good morning." A hospice nurse with warm brown eyes and a smile to match ushered them into the living room.

Macy wandered in, looking as forlorn as they'd ever seen her. "Hi, Max."

"We gotta kitten," he said.

"I know." Macy smiled. "I've seen them in the barn. You know which one is my favorite? The little orange calico with the black patch over her eye."

Lucas could tell by the look on Erin's face that she'd had no idea the little girl *had* a favorite. But the slow smile that drew up the corner of her lips was a sure sign that Max had chosen the right one.

Max jumped up and down. "That's the one we bringed."

Macy looked to Erin for an explanation.

"I don't think we're going to be able to keep this a secret very long," she laughed. "Max, why don't you take Macy into the kitchen and introduce her to her Christmas present?"

Max didn't need to be asked twice. He grabbed the older girl by the hand and ran from the room.

Darlene Perry lay in a hospital bed, her features ravaged by the disease that had slowly won the battle. "Come in and sit down."

Lucas looked at Jonathan, who nodded. "I have to make a phone call. I'll be back in a few minutes."

Jonathan excused himself from the room while Lucas and Erin took a seat on the worn sofa.

"Sweet of you, Erin," Darlene rasped, her breathing labored. "Macy talks about your animals all the time."

"I enjoy having her visit."

"Brooke said she would stop by this morning." Darlene's head rolled toward the window. "She and Zach are going to pick Macy up later this afternoon and take her skating."

Lucas cleared his throat, wondering how much he should say. "I'm sure Brooke will be here, but Zach has to…work."

Darlene's sunken eyes clouded. "Did something happen?"

Lucas hesitated. He didn't want to cause undue stress on Darlene, yet it seemed to him there'd been enough secrets in the family. Like Reverend West had said in his sermon, maybe it was time to let some light in.

"He had to arrest his aunt, Katrina Clayton, last night. It turns out that she was responsible for planning the attacks against my family the past few months."

Darlene began to tremble violently and Erin went to her side. Lucas inwardly kicked himself.

"I'm sorry, Mrs. Perry." Once again, it appeared he'd made the wrong decision.

"No." Darlene gasped. "I'm glad you told me. I thought I was doing the right thing...I made a promise." Her legs moved restlessly beneath the blankets.

Erin took Darlene's hand and comforted her in the same way she'd comforted Max.

"Is there anything we can do?" Lucas asked, feeling responsible for causing the woman more pain.

"Call Reverend West," Darlene whispered. "And the rest of your family. They need to...hear."

Lucas wasn't sure he understood. "My family?"

"Yes...ask them to come." Darlene struggled to sit up. "Soon."

"All right." Lucas met Jonathan in the doorway and pulled him aside. "Darlene wants Reverend

West here. And the rest of the family. I'm not sure that's a good idea—"

"Yes, it is," the doctor interrupted. "Something has been weighing on that poor woman since I met her. If I were you, I'd do what she said. As soon as possible."

That was all Lucas needed to hear. "I'll start making phone calls."

Chapter Twenty

One by one, cars began to line up along the snow-covered driveway as the Clayton family gathered in Darlene Perry's living room.

The festive Christmas decorations were at odds with the somber mood. Reverend West moved from couple to couple, his presence easing the tension that had begun to permeate the air as members of the family arrived.

"I asked you all to come here today…" Darlene looked at Reverend West, who nodded encouragingly. "I made a promise ten years ago. I shouldn't have…but I thought I had to keep it. I didn't know if it was right but I prayed about it. When Lucas told me about Kat, it was an answer to my prayer."

Gabe slipped his arm around Brooke's shoulders. The gesture wasn't lost on Darlene. Tears pooled in her eyes.

"I don't want this to cause anyone pain…I want it to bring healing. What Kat did…it was wrong. What

I did was wrong, too. I hope she finds the forgiveness that I have." Darlene released a ragged breath. "Ten years ago, I had an affair…"

Across the room, Mei's eyes met Lucas's. He braced himself to hear his father's name, suddenly grateful their mother wasn't in the room. It would be better hearing the news from one of them rather than from Darlene.

"With George Clayton Jr."

Brooke's audible gasp sounded like a gunshot in the quiet room. Vivienne turned her face into Cody's broad shoulder. Zach didn't look surprised by the admission, leaving Lucas to wonder if he hadn't suspected this all along.

"It's all right," Reverend West murmured. "Take your time."

Darlene nodded, tears tracking her hollow cheeks. "Georgie and I dated in high school, but your grandfather said I wasn't good enough for him. No one stood up to George Clayton Sr., so he broke up with me."

"Your father—" Her gaze touched on Zach, Brooke and Vivienne. "He loved you—and your mother. George was going through a difficult time after Lucy died and he turned to me for comfort. It was a mistake. We both knew that. When I found out I was pregnant, neither of us knew what to do. George didn't want to lose his family, but he was a good man. He wanted to do the right thing."

Darlene's gaze bounced from Mei to Lucas. Lucas

sucked in a breath, knowing that somehow this situation involved his father, too.

"He confided in his brother. Vern was…furious. He didn't want a scandal in the family."

Bitterness swelled in Lucas. Of course his father hadn't wanted a scandal. His reputation had become the most important thing in his life, more important than his family or even the God he served.

"Uncle Vern and my dad were on their way to your house when the accident happened, weren't they?" Vivienne asked in the silence that followed.

"I think so." Everyone had to strain to hear Darlene now. "After they died, I didn't know what to do. I finally got the courage to tell your grandfather. He didn't want to have anything to do with me or the baby."

Reverend West moved to Darlene's side and took her hand, giving her the strength to continue. She gave the minister a grateful look. "George offered me money if I kept the name of Macy's father a secret. I didn't know what else to do. I was pregnant and alone. George Jr. was gone. I didn't want to cause your family any more grief—your mother deserved the good memories she had of her husband. It wouldn't have been right to take those away."

"You had to think of Macy," Brooke said. Her face was as white as Darlene's, but already the warm light of forgiveness kindled in her eyes.

"Where does Kat fit into all this?" Zach asked, his expression still guarded.

Lucas had harbored no illusions about his father, but this had to be tough on his older cousin, too. George Jr. and Zach hadn't been close, either, but the news of his father's infidelity still had to cut deep.

"I thought a woman might be more sympathetic to my situation," Darlene confessed. "I met with Kat and poured out my heart to her. She said she would see what she could do—but what she did was look out for herself."

"She tried to extort money from her own father." Arabella, who had been silent up until now, dashed at the tears welling up in her eyes. "She wanted cash in exchange for her silence."

"Yes." Darlene took a sip of water from the glass Laura West offered her. "Kat left town after that. I bought this house with the money George Sr. gave me and raised Macy the best I could. When I got sick, I knew that my daughter would need a family. I prayed about what to do. I didn't want to hurt anyone, but Macy needed you. All of you. I'm so sorry to cause you more pain."

"I'm sorry, Darlene." Arabella moved across the room and sat down next to Macy's mother. "Sorry for what my mother did. Sorry the family wasn't there for Macy—or for you—a long time ago. If we'd known, we could have helped."

A murmur of agreement rippled around the room.

"You may not agree with George's methods, but his motives were good," Reverend West said. "He acknowledged his mistakes and got right with God." A hint of a smile touched the man's lips now. "I think as far as the will is concerned, George would say that the end justified the means. You're all in Clayton. Now each one of you has to decide where to go from here."

Darlene's head rolled back against the pillow. "George wanted to make things right before he died. I—I wanted to do the same thing. If it isn't too late."

"It's never too late." Arabella leaned down and embraced Darlene. Vivienne and Brooke followed suit, offering the forgiveness that Darlene longed for.

Watching his cousins, Lucas felt the last of his defenses crumble. In spite of Kat's negative influence, Arabella was a wonderful mother to her girls. If she could overcome the past, maybe he could, too.

Darlene's eyes fluttered closed, and Jonathan quickly moved to her side. "I think Darlene should rest now."

Arabella looked at him, a question in her eyes. Jonathan nodded and took Darlene's hand. The woman's peaceful smile rivaled the lights on the Christmas tree. "You'll all stay...for a while?" she asked in a broken whisper.

Brooke smiled through her tears. "We're family. I'm afraid you're stuck with us."

It was almost eight o'clock when the headlights from Lucas's truck cut a swath through the darkness.

"Daddy's here?" Max looked up from the puzzle they'd been putting together.

Ever since Max's stay in the hospital, he no longer called Lucas by his first name. That day had been a turning point for both of them.

"I think so." Erin brushed the curtain aside, her heart in her throat. It had been a difficult afternoon, waiting for him to return. Wondering why Darlene had asked Lucas's family to gather at her home.

She and Max had eaten supper hours ago. When the house began to cool, Erin started a fire and supervised Max while he took a bubble bath.

Erin had been drawing the bedtime routine out, hoping Lucas would make it home before she tucked Max in bed for the night.

Max heard Lucas's footsteps and bounded to the door. "Weputapuzzletogetherandplayedgamesandbuiltatower…"

"Whoa. Take a breath, bud. My ears can't keep up." Lucas flashed a weary grin before turning to Erin. "I'm sorry I'm late. Again."

"It's all right. Max and I have been having fun."

Lucas picked up his son and hugged him until he squirmed. "I can't breathe, Daddy!"

"I know it's a little past his bedtime, but he wanted to see you before he fell asleep."

"I wanted to see him, too." Lucas fumbled with the buttons on his coat. Without thinking, Erin brushed his cold hands aside and took over, unfastening them the way she would have done if it were Max standing in front of her.

"I'm gonna brush my teeth and pick out a story." Max scrambled up the stairs.

Erin waited until she heard the bathroom door close. "Darlene?"

"She passed away an hour ago."

Tears sprang into her eyes. "Was Macy…?"

"Not at the end. It was what Darlene wanted. They spent some time together and then Jasmine and Cade took her and the triplets and A.J. Wesson back to Arabella's house. The rest of us stayed with her."

The lump in Erin's throat expanded. "It must have been so hard to say goodbye to her daughter."

"Yes…and no." Lucas cleared his throat. "She was an amazing woman. Darlene told us that she had peace knowing she would be safe in the Lord's arms and Macy…Macy would be safe in ours."

Lucas reached out and brushed a tear off her cheek with the pad of his thumb. "That was everyone's response," he murmured.

Erin knew there was more he wanted to say, but Max galloped down the stairs and flew into Lucas's arms. "Can we open a present tonight?"

"I'll tell you what." Lucas tucked Max under his arm like a football. "Saturday night is Christmas Eve. You can open one present after Jasmine and Cade's wedding. How does that sound?"

Max's face lit up. "Really?"

"Really. Now up to bed."

"Are you going to open one, too?" Max asked.

"Sure."

"Is Erin goin' to open one?" Max looked concerned.

"Erin's presents are under her tree at home," Lucas pointed out.

Max thought about that. "You can open one anyway," he whispered. "Santa won't mind."

"I just might do that." Erin swept Max into her arms and planted a kiss on top of his head, breathing in the scent of bubblegum shampoo.

"Okay." His little feet barely touched the floor when he danced up the stairs.

"Darlene wanted a small, private memorial service," Lucas said. "Reverend West is making the arrangements for the day after tomorrow. She made Arabella promise that Jasmine and Cade wouldn't postpone the wedding. Darlene said it was another step toward healing for our family—and for Macy."

"I wish I would have known her better," Erin murmured. "She must have been a very strong woman."

"So is Arabella, considering what she's been through the past few days. Finding out her mother was behind everything hasn't been easy on her."

Erin nodded. "I know. We've been working almost round the clock to get things ready. Kylie, Vivienne and I are finishing up the food tomorrow."

"But aren't you going to the wedding?"

"Since I'm not family, I offered to take charge of the reception dinner. I'm needed more there."

Something in Lucas's expression caused Erin's breath to catch in her throat. "But I need—"

"Daddy!" Max appeared at the top of the stairs. "I found a book about a cowboy!"

Erin smiled. "I'll let myself out."

"Are you sure you don't want to stay longer?"

"I'm sure." Erin turned down the invitation even as she silently acknowledged the truth.

She *wanted* to stay. Forever.

Chapter Twenty-One

Luminaries lined the snow-covered sidewalk as the wedding guests arrived.

Over the course of the day, Clayton Christian Church had been turned into the setting of a fairy-tale wedding with hundreds of tiny lights, lush poinsettias, white roses and miles of white netting.

Lucas saw Kylie slip in through the front doors and join Zach in the foyer. There was no sign of Erin. He'd been lurking in the hallway for almost half an hour, hoping she'd changed her mind about attending the ceremony.

"Is Erin still setting up the buffet?" He had to ask.

Kylie's pert nose wrinkled. "She made me leave but she insisted on staying to keep an eye on the food. She said, and I quote, 'I'm your boss so you have to do what I say.' Unquote."

"She should be here," Lucas muttered.

Kylie gave him a look. "Then convince her. I'll keep an eye on Max for a few minutes."

Lucas was out the door and across the street to the town hall, already formulating a list of reasons why Erin should attend the wedding.

I'm not part of the family, she'd said.

Well, if Lucas had his way, she wouldn't be able to say that again after tonight.

He pushed open the door and saw her fussing with a centerpiece on the table. A white apron skimmed her trim frame but couldn't completely conceal the filmy black dress that clung to her slender curves. Instead of a ponytail, silver filigree combs caught up her hair in a loose topknot.

"You look beautiful."

Erin started at the sound of his voice. "Isn't the ceremony about to start?" she asked, a blush staining her cheeks.

"That's why I'm here. Come on."

She balked. "I can't. I've got to stay—"

"Everything looks great. And it will still look great a half hour from now when the reception starts." Lucas took a step toward her and Erin took a step back.

"Max was asking where you were." Okay, so it was low to use his son to get his way, but Lucas knew Max wouldn't mind. And he *had* been asking about Erin.

"I suppose." Erin started to fumble with the strings on her apron and Lucas gently pushed her hands aside.

"Let me." He worked the knot free, overwhelmed by the urge to take her into his arms again.

But then they'd both be late for the wedding…

Five minutes later, they were seated in the back of the church, Max perched on his lap and Erin at his side.

Jack and one of Cade's friends from high school took their place at the front of the church next to Reverend West. Most of the groom's family was missing—Lucas had heard that Samuel and a few key members of his family had taken an extended vacation—but the George Clayton side was there in full force.

As the prelude began, Arabella's triplets, adorable in emerald-green velvet, danced up the aisle, each carrying a basket of rose petals. Macy followed at a more sedate pace, the hem of her satin gown swishing around her ankles.

"There's Julie an' Jamie an' Jessie!" Max sang out before Lucas could shush him.

Erin bit her lip to keep from smiling as laughter rippled through the church.

Everyone rose to their feet as Jonathan and Jasmine appeared in the doorway. The young bride looked stunning in a floor-length gown glistening with seed pearls. A veil covered Jasmine's face but Lucas could see her wide smile beneath it.

"Please be seated." Reverend West came to stand in front of the bride and groom and opened a small leather Bible. "I'd like to read from the book of Isaiah this evening.

"'Therefore the Lord himself will give you a sign. The virgin will be with child and will give birth to a son, and will call him Emmanuel,' which means God with us.

"This is a familiar passage read at Christmastime, but maybe you're wondering why I chose to read it tonight, as Jasmine and Cade exchange their wedding vows."

Reverend West closed the Bible and his warm smile encompassed the people who were listening. "Because both are about promises. Tonight, Jasmine and Cade are making promises to each other. To love one another. To forgive one another. To forsake all others. Love is more than a feeling—it's a promise.

"In Isaiah, almost seven hundred years before Jesus was born, God promised the world a Savior— His only son. God promises He will never forsake us. Never. Emmanuel. God *with* us. The promise of that first Christmas." Reverend West nodded at the young couple. "With God as the center of your marriage, you will be able to get through the ups and downs that every couple faces as they journey together. He'll help you keep the promises you make tonight—because He's a God who keeps His."

He gave Cade a reassuring nod as tears streamed down Jasmine's face. Cade took her hand and offered a watery smile of his own.

Reverend West smiled. "Let's pray and ask God's blessing on this young couple."

Lucas finally cornered Erin after the reception meal. Her cheeks were flushed and tendrils of hair had escaped from the combs, but she had never looked lovelier.

"I think we're going to call it a night." Lucas hoisted a giggling Max over his shoulder. "Would you like to stop over for a while?"

"Max is probably tired. And he's going to have a busy day tomorrow."

Lucas hiked a brow. "Does Max *look* tired?"

As if to underscore the point, Max wiggled around until he was facing her. "You haveta watch me open my present."

"I wouldn't want to miss that."

There were a lot of things Lucas didn't want to miss, either. Like every moment with Erin.

"So, that's a yes?" Lucas prodded gently.

"Sure." Erin smiled at Max. "Arabella hired a cleanup crew, so I don't think they need me anymore."

That was good. Because *he* needed her.

Erin's car pulled in a few minutes after his. Max had brushed his teeth and prepared for bed in record time. Lucas put on an instrumental Christmas CD and pulled a plate of cookies Arabella had given him out of the freezer.

He was as nervous as the proverbial cat on a hot

tin roof when Erin walked in. Max didn't have the same issues. He raced over to Erin, grabbed her hand and tugged her toward the Christmas tree, his patience finally at an end. Lucas knew the feeling!

Max flopped down and retrieved a lumpy package. "This one's yours." He handed it to Lucas. "A'bella helped me wrap it."

Lucas carefully opened the present under Max's watchful eye. Inside was a framed photograph of him and Max…and Erin. One of his sneaky cousins must have snapped it at the reception.

"That's…" Erin's voice trailed off in a squeak.

Max leaned in to see what all the fuss was about. "Us," he said matter-of-factly.

"Which one are you going to open?" Her cheeks pink, Erin redirected the attention back to the gifts.

"This one!" Max wrapped both arms around the largest present and hauled it out from under the tree. He unwrapped it and tunneled through a thick layer of red tissue paper.

"Cowboy boots!"

"Every cowboy needs one to go with his hat," his dad said.

Max hurtled himself into Lucas's lap. "I love them." The tip of his nose touched Lucas's and brought them eyeball to eyeball. "I. Love. You."

"I love you, too." Lucas somehow managed to get the words out.

"Where's Erin's?" Max tilted his head, looking at Lucas expectantly.

"I don't—"

Lucas cut her off with a smile. "It's the one with the pink bow."

The one with the pink bow?

Erin slanted a look at Lucas, feeling self-conscious. She didn't want him to feel obligated to give her a present because he'd allowed Max to open one.

"It's a new tradition. One present on Christmas Eve," Lucas said.

"Yup." Max nodded vigorously. "You gotta open it."

"All right." Erin slid her fingernail through the tape and unwrapped layers of gold paper until she found a plain pine...box. Obviously old. And judging by the whittle marks in the wood, handmade.

She gave Lucas a questioning look.

"It belonged to my great-grandfather, Jim Clayton," Lucas explained. "Grandpa George gave it to me when I was twelve years old. I have to admit, I was disappointed."

"So you...regifted it?"

"In a way." Lucas didn't smile in response to her teasing. "I didn't appreciate what it meant at the time. Grandpa George said he was passing it on to me because I would understand it's value. It took me long enough, but now I do.

"In his will, my grandfather asked each of us to think of one good memory of him. I realized it was the day he gave me this gift because it reminded me of what was important."

Erin couldn't hide her confusion. "If it's a family heirloom, shouldn't you keep it?"

Lucas shook his head. "My cousins think God brought us back here to reconnect with our roots, but I don't believe that."

Erin's heart sank. "You don't?"

"I've been thinking—and praying—about this a lot over the past few days. And I believe God brought me back to Clayton for *you,* Erin. Because He meant for us to be together." Lucas took the box from her numb fingers and opened the lid.

Tucked in a nest of gold tissue paper was another box. A very small, velvet box.

Erin couldn't move. Couldn't breathe. Couldn't speak.

"You got another one, Erin!" Max wiggled closer. "Open it!"

But she *still* couldn't move. So Lucas lifted the cover. When he did, a diamond solitaire winked at her from its setting in a simple gold band.

"Erin Fields, I love you more than life itself," he said softly. "Will you marry me and make me the happiest man on earth?"

She couldn't speak, either.

"Why's Erin cryin', Daddy?" Max said with a worried frown.

"I'm not sure." Lucas sounded just as worried.

Erin decided it was time to put their fears to rest.

And hers, too. Their lives may have taken different paths for a few years, but Lucas was right. God had brought them back together.

"They're happy tears," she sniffled.

Max frowned. "What's that mean?"

Laughing, Erin launched herself into Lucas's arms with the same enthusiasm that Max had just moments ago.

"Yes," she whispered in his ear. "It means yes."

Epilogue

Christmas Eve—One Year Later

"Are you sure you're ready for this?" Lucas pulled up in front of Clayton House and managed to squeeze his pickup between a minivan and the deputy sheriff's car parked along the curb. "My family can be a little overwhelming, you know."

He didn't fool her a bit. Erin heard the undercurrent of deep affection in the teasing comment. "They're your family, Lucas. I love every single one of them."

"That's good." Lucas muttered. "Because every single one of them is here tonight."

"'Cause it's Jesus' birthday tomorrow," Max piped up from the backseat. "And we're goin' to have a party and cake and everything!"

"You're right, buddy. And I can't think of a better way to celebrate." Lucas wove his fingers through Erin's and gave them a warm squeeze, sending her pulse into a little skip. "Unless it's sitting in front of a blazing fire with my beautiful wife," he murmured.

"That part comes later," Erin promised in a whisper.

Lucas helped her out of the truck before releasing Max from his booster seat. He sprinted up the path, the old black Stetson bouncing on his head and his cowboy boots churning up the snow.

Right before they'd left, Max had appeared at the top of the stairs wearing the pair of black corduroy pants and a crisp plaid shirt Erin had bought him for the evening service—and Lucas's old cowboy hat. Erin hadn't asked him to take it off. She'd taken his picture for next year's Christmas card instead.

The door flew open before they reached the top step. The triplets surrounded Max and for a moment Erin lost sight of him in the sudden flurry of sparkling taffeta and ruffles.

"Max, come see the birthday cake Auntie Viv made," Jessie said, grabbing her younger cousin by the hand.

"It's got lotsa frosting." A.J. Wesson, adorable in a white shirt and a necktie sprinkled with tiny gingerbread men, spun in a circle and almost took out the coatrack. "Macy helped dec'rate it."

Max paused long enough to shed his coat before chasing after his cousins through an obstacle course of discarded boots, hats and gloves.

"I think we better watch Max's sugar intake this evening or he'll be up all night," Lucas said.

"You're such a dad." Erin slipped her arm around his waist.

Lucas took advantage of the moment to turn her fully into his arms, dip her backward and press a kiss against her soft pink lips.

"Uncle Lucas and Auntie Erin are kissin' again!" Jamie announced as she scampered past.

"That's because they're newlyweds," Jasmine said when Erin and Lucas stepped into the living room.

Erin blushed. "We've been married eight months," she protested.

In spite of the number of engagements over the past year, she and Lucas had been the first couple to exchange vows after Jasmine and Cade's Christmas Eve wedding.

Lucas had informed his cousins they would have to wait their turn because he and Erin, with their "seven-year courtship," had been together the longest.

Erin knew exactly what he meant. Their love had never died—it had simply remained stored in their hearts until God had brought them back together again.

And Lucas Clayton had been worth the wait.

He and Max had moved into her house after the wedding and when Tweed retired, Lucas had taken over the practice. The first thing he'd done was hire a partner and a vet tech so that he could spend more time at home with his wife and adopted son.

It was one of the many changes Erin had seen in her husband. Little by little, Clayton's prodigal son had been drawn back into the fold. He'd even coached a boy's T-ball team the previous summer at the Lucy Clayton Recreational Center that Brooke had opened in memory of her sister.

"It's our first anniversary," Cade reminded them. "So technically, we are no longer newlyweds."

"I suppose that makes you an old married couple?" Lucas swept a herd of plastic horses aside to make room on the sofa.

"Of course," Jasmine said. "We can give the rest of you advice!"

A collective groan followed the cheerful statement.

"I knew we shouldn't have let them get married so young," Arabella told Jonathan in a stage whisper. "And they've got six months on us."

Arabella and Jasmine's uncle had married in June, the month Jonathan had officially relocated his practice from Denver to Clayton. Jasmine and Cade had stayed in the city while he attended college and she attended culinary school, but the couple often came home on weekends to visit.

"And four on Brooke and I," Gabe added. "So if seniority rules, we can give Mei and Jack advice. They aren't getting married until Valentine's Day."

"What are we talking about?" Vivienne swept

into the living room with a cheese tray. She paused long enough to let Cody snag a handful of crackers.

"Weddings." Zach sighed but his eyes were twinkling. "What else?"

"And in spite of what *some* people might think," Mei looked pointedly at the men in the room, "they are not a competition."

Cody crossed his arms. "Everything is a competition."

"He's right." Jack grinned. "And we're going to come in dead last." He looked at Mei and lowered his voice to a stage whisper. "Unless we elope tonight."

"No way." Kylie entered the fray. "No one elopes on my watch. I love planning weddings and no one is going to cheat me out of the opportunity!"

"See what you started?" Arabella smiled at her foster daughter. "A whole *stampede* of Clayton weddings."

Jasmine performed a cute little curtsey. "You're all very welcome."

Brooke looped one arm around Gabe and the other around Macy. "I wonder if Grandpa George knew what he was starting when he wrote up that will."

"Oh, I think he *hoped*," Mei said softly.

The smile she and Lucas exchanged warmed Erin's heart.

Even though the conditions of the will had recently been met and everyone had received their inheritance, the past twelve months had connected the family in ways no one had quite expected.

George's will might have forced them to return to Clayton, but it was their love for each other that made it *home.*

"Are you looking for another piece of cake, Lucas?" Vivienne held up a plate.

Lucas winced and patted his flat stomach. "If I eat another piece of cake, I'll have to roll myself to the church. Actually, I'm looking for Erin."

He'd lost track of his wife at some point between the children's roof-raising Happy Birthday chorus and the cake-cutting, picture-taking, cleaning-frosting-off-the-walls event that followed.

"I think she went thataway." Vivienne pointed a chef's knife in the direction of the small sitting room located off the kitchen.

The room was washed in shadows, the only light coming from the streetlight shining through the window. Lucas started to back up when he saw a faint glimmer of copper.

Concern propelled him across the room. He dropped to his knees in front of the chair Erin was sitting in.

"What's the matter?"

"Nothing at all," Erin said quickly. "I'm just feeling a little tired tonight, I guess. It's been a busy week."

"I heard A.J. tell Brooke that the triplets were

making his *ears* tired." Lucas was rewarded with a wan smile. "A family get-together can have that effect on people."

"I love your family."

"I know, but at times like this, don't you wish it were smaller?"

"Not for a moment." Erin paused and a smile played at the corners of her lips. "Do you ever wish it were bigger?"

Something in her eyes made Lucas catch his breath. "Erin?"

She looped her arms around his neck. "My Christmas present to you is that by this time next year, Max will have a brother or a sister."

His heart expanding at the unexpected news, all Lucas could do was stare at her. A baby. By next Christmas.

"I know we didn't plan on having a baby so soon." Erin bit her lip. "You aren't upset, are you?"

"Are you kidding? You know what this means, don't you?"

"What?"

A slow smile spread across Lucas's face. "We're in the lead again."

* * * * *

Dear Reader,

I enjoyed being part of the Rocky Mountain Heirs series because it combines two things that are very special to me—faith and family.

Proverbs 13:22 says, *"A good man leaves an inheritance for his children's children..."* That's what Lucas's grandfather, George Clayton, wanted to do. He took steps near the end of his life to make sure his family could have a new start. A new start that involved forgiveness, commitment and, of course, love!

It's my prayer that after reading this series, you will have a new and deeper appreciation for your own family. With God's help, we can all leave a wonderful legacy to the next generation.

I love to hear from my readers! Check out my website at www.kathrynspringer.com and sign up to receive my free quarterly newsletter. And until we meet again in the pages of my next book, keep smiling...and seeking Him!

Blessings,

Kathryn Springer

Questions for Discussion

1. Did you support or disagree with George Clayton Sr.'s plan to convince his grandchildren to return to Clayton? What was his motivation?

2. What factors influenced Lucas's decision to leave Colorado at the age of eighteen? How did they compare to Erin's reasons for staying?

3. The Clayton family had been divided for years because of a long-standing feud between George Sr. and his brother Samuel. How did this affect other relationships? Have you ever experienced this kind of difficulty in your family? What did you do to solve it?

4. Whether real or imagined, both Erin and Lucas struggled with the expectations their families placed on them. How did they respond? Which of them can you relate to the most in that regard?

5. What qualities did Erin possess that Lucas admired? Why do you think she didn't see those things in herself?

6. It was clear from the moment they met that Erin and Lucas still had feelings for one another, but what was the turning point in their relationship?

7. Lucas felt inadequate when it came to being a good father to Max. If you are a parent, what is the issue you struggle with the most? What is an area in which you feel confident when it comes to raising your children?

8. Erin's mother told her to "look for the good" that was right in front of her. Do you think that was good advice? What does it mean to you?

9. In what ways did Macy Perry bring the Clayton family back together?

10. Katrina Clayton allowed a root of bitterness to grow in her heart. Compare and contrast her character to Darlene Perry, who turned to God to find healing. What lessons can we learn from these two women?

11. How did you feel about Jasmine and Cade marrying so young? What are some of the challenges they might face? What will they need to overcome them?

12. When did you figure out who was responsible for the attacks on the Clayton family? What hints led you to that conclusion?

13. Which couple in the Rocky Mountain Heirs continuity series did you relate to the most? Why?

14. What was your favorite scene? Why?

15. What does the word *legacy* mean to you? What kind of legacy do you want to pass on to the next generation? What steps will you take to do this?

LARGER-PRINT BOOKS!

**GET 2 FREE
LARGER-PRINT NOVELS
PLUS 2 FREE
MYSTERY GIFTS**

Larger-print novels are now available...

YES! Please send me 2 FREE LARGER-PRINT Love Inspired® novels and my 2 FREE mystery gifts (gifts are worth about $10). After receiving them, if I don't wish to receive any more books, I can return the shipping statement marked "cancel". If I don't cancel, I will receive 6 brand-new novels every month and be billed just $4.99 per book in the U.S. or $5.49 per book in Canada. That's a saving of at least 23% off the cover price. It's quite a bargain! Shipping and handling is just 50¢ per book in the U.S. and 75¢ per book in Canada.* I understand that accepting the 2 free books and gifts places me under no obligation to buy anything. I can always return a shipment and cancel at any time. Even if I never buy another book, the two free books and gifts are mine to keep forever.

122/322 IDN FEG3

Name _____ (PLEASE PRINT) _____

Address _____ Apt. # _____

City _____ State/Prov. _____ Zip/Postal Code _____

Signature (if under 18, a parent or guardian must sign)

Mail to the **Reader Service:**
IN U.S.A.: P.O. Box 1867, Buffalo, NY 14240-1867
IN CANADA: P.O. Box 609, Fort Erie, Ontario L2A 5X3

Not valid to current subscribers to Love Inspired Larger-Print books.

**Are you a current subscriber to Love Inspired books
and want to receive the larger-print edition?
Call 1-800-873-8635 or visit www.ReaderService.com.**

* Terms and prices subject to change without notice. Prices do not include applicable taxes. Sales tax applicable in N.Y. Canadian residents will be charged applicable taxes. Offer not valid in Quebec. This offer is limited to one order per household. All orders subject to credit approval. Credit or debit balances in a customer's account(s) may be offset by any other outstanding balance owed by or to the customer. Please allow 4 to 6 weeks for delivery. Offer available while quantities last.

Your Privacy—The Reader Service is committed to protecting your privacy. Our Privacy Policy is available online at www.ReaderService.com or upon request from the Reader Service.

We make a portion of our mailing list available to reputable third parties that offer products we believe may interest you. If you prefer that we not exchange your name with third parties, or if you wish to clarify or modify your communication preferences, please visit us at www.ReaderService.com/consumerchoice or write to us at Reader Service Preference Service, P.O. Box 9062, Buffalo, NY 14269. Include your complete name and address.

LILPI1B

Love Inspired®
SUSPENSE
RIVETING INSPIRATIONAL ROMANCE

Watch for our series of edge-
of-your-seat suspense novels.
These contemporary tales
of intrigue and romance
feature Christian characters
facing challenges to their faith...
and their lives!

AVAILABLE IN REGULAR
& LARGER-PRINT FORMATS

For exciting stories that reflect traditional values,
visit:
www.ReaderService.com